M000187464

PAST, PRESENT, and FUTURE

an ARIA Anthology

Selected short fiction, non-fiction, poetry & prose
from The Association of Rhode Island Authors

Past, Present, and Future: Selected Short Fiction, Non-fiction Poetry and Prose from The Association of Rhode Island Authors. ©2019 Association of Rhode Island Authors. Entries are ©2019 to their respective authors. All selections have been included with the authors' consent. Produced and printed by Stillwater River Publications. All rights reserved. Written and produced in the United States of America. This book may not be reproduced or sold in any form without the expressed, written permission of the authors and publisher.

Visit our website at www.StillwaterPress.com for more information.

First Stillwater River Publications Edition

Library of Congress Control Number: 2019954913

ISBN-13: 978-1-950339-57-0

1 2 3 4 5 6 7 8 9 10
A publication of the Association of Rhode Island Authors (ARIA)
Cover Design by Emma St. Jean.
Published by Stillwater River Publications, Pawtucket, RI, USA.

The views and opinions expressed in this book are solely those of the individual authors and do not necessarily reflect the views and opinions of the Association of Rhode Island Authors (ARIA) or the publisher.

Table of Contents

Introduction

This is the fourth annual anthology of works from the Association of Rhode Island Authors, a three-hundred-plus member group of poets and writers. With no theme attached to this year's anthology, our writers were unrestricted in their choice of work to submit for consideration.

Past, Present, and Future is just what the title implies: a variety of prose and poetry that looks back, forward, and straight ahead. With recollections and memories, we remember – sometimes with regret, sometimes with a smile. By focusing on the present, we are influenced by that which is immediately around us. And with eyes to the future, we must imagine what life could be, whether full of hope or steeped in anxiety.

If you've read through any of the previous anthologies, you know the talent that exists in our group of writers and poets. You know the variety of work you'll find in this compendium, the joy of finding the work of someone you know personally, or meeting a new writer and realizing you must read more! If you're featured in this anthology, perhaps for the first time, congratulations! You are now published. That's an accomplishment worth sharing with everyone you know.

I was honored to serve as chair for this anthology. It was by seeing the variety of works submitted by our authors that I was reminded of the talent that exists in this extraordinary group. Our panel of volunteer judges took on the difficult task of reading and reviewing dozens of submissions, and determining the final anthology.

Enjoy reading through *Past, Present, and Future* – at your leisure, with your feet up, perhaps in the coming months when winter tells us we should read more. And if your emotions are stirred by a particular story or poem, feel free to share your thoughts!

Martha Reynolds, Editor

Under a Metamorphosis Moon

Paul Magnan

I t was three minutes after midnight. The full moon blazed through every window, insistent, hunting. In a corner untouched by the seeking light, I held her.

I wiped Mo's face. Iridescent sparkles faded as her sweat evaporated from the tissue.

She opened her eyes, two silver orbs bright in the darkness. "Gary."

I took her hand. The moon ran like an electric current beneath her skin. "I'm here."

Mo coughed. A splatter of silver coated her lips. Still she smiled. "Take me outside. Please."

Tears formed in my eyes, and I wiped them away. The moist streaks glowed on my hand.

* * *

When it was first spotted, astronomers thought it was a comet. It had a definable head and, as it streaked through space toward the sun, it grew the classic flared tail. But as it approached, they discovered there was no ice or rock in the nucleus. There was no matter at all. It was a ball of unknown energy.

No alarm bells were rung, at least not in the early days. Not even when it was determined that the anomaly, for there was no other name for it, would pass very close to earth. As it got closer its speed increased, which was normal for regular comets with solid cores, but there was nothing within the anomaly to react to the sun's gravitational pull.

It was soon determined that the earth's moon was directly in its path. Scientists tried to play this down by announcing that the energy content in the head of the anomaly would not physically damage or alter the moon's orbit in any way, that if anything, nothing more than a spectacular light show would be the result. In truth, nobody knew what the effect of the coming collision would be.

There were a few doomsday prophets, of course, but on the whole, there was no panic. People put their faith in the reassurances of the scientific community and carried on with their lives.

The collision occurred on July 8 at 02:37 GMT, during a full moon that shone over much of Europe, Africa, western Asia, and the eastern halves of North and South America.

Mo and I watched it on television. There were numerous "light show" parties in many cities witnessing the event, but the skies over our Rhode Island home were overcast, and we were disappointed not to be able to watch from our own yard.

The anomaly approached the moon at what seemed to be slow-motion speed, although on-air astronomers assured viewers it was moving very quickly. To me, it looked like the few comets I had seen, hazy white with a distinctive tail. It was less than half the size of the moon, and when it struck, the world held its breath and…nothing happened.

"Did it go behind the moon?" Mo asked. I shrugged, my eyes locked on the television.

A moment later the moon exploded.

Bright orange light shot outward. Screams of horror, filtered through our television, ripped from the throats of multitudes. Mo's mouth hung open in shock. I imagine my own expression could not have been any better. What would happen, I wondered, now that the powerful gravitational dance between the earth and the moon was over? Would the ocean, mere miles away, buck and roil like a gigantic, maddened horse and swallow us under billions of gallons of water?

These initial thoughts of doom faded into relief when the television picture cleared and showed that the moon was still there. It appeared to be in one piece, and while I am no expert on the moon, I couldn't discern any changes upon its surface. The only difference I could see was that it seemed to shine brighter than it did before. Scientists assured the world that there was no need to be afraid, that nothing untoward had happened.

* * *

On the night after the collision, grass glowed silver, making lawns and fields appear phantasmal. Leaves shone with silver veins, giving wooded areas the appearance of magical wonderlands.

Mo was enchanted. She went out and bathed herself in the unnaturally bright full moon, dancing in our silver-drenched back lawn like a victorious faerie queen. We owned twelve acres of land and had no close neighbors, which made me very glad when Mo suddenly shed her clothes and stood naked in the argent grass. She raised her face and arms up to the moon and smiled, her bare skin drinking in the light like ambrosia. She shivered in ecstasy.

Anxiety twisted my stomach. I called to Mo and begged her to come inside. She laughed and skipped away, as if daring me to come out and catch her.

Mo returned three hours later. She brushed past me without speaking and went to bed. Within seconds she was asleep.

Soon after that, the sun flared above the eastern horizon. The glow of the plants faded away, leaving them their normal green. But I suspected the silver phosphorescence was still there, hiding away, dormant, biding its time before the sunlight dipped away and the moon once more held reign over the sky.

* * *

A week later the plants began to liquefy and seep into the ground.

I watched through the back window as stalks of grass, under the last quarter moon, melted like candle wax and drained into the earth. In the wooded areas, leaves dripped off branches, and deep in the crevices of trunks, wood pulp deliquesced and ran out in thick, luminous strands.

"It's so beautiful, isn't it?"

I jumped. I hadn't heard Mo approach.

"The plants are dying. The moon has done something to them."

"No," Mo smiled at me. "It's the start of the call."

I looked at her. I couldn't form a coherent question to ask what she meant.

"Look," Mo said, pointing out the window.

A wild rabbit wandered into our yard. Although moonlight blasted as bright as a distant searchlight, a silver glow could be discerned from the rabbit's eyes and mouth as it stumbled in the melting grass.

"Watch." The rapture in Mo's voice frightened me more than the awful dissolution happening outside.

The rabbit swayed on its feet. Its body rose and fell with rapid hitches as it desperately drew in air. After a minute it stilled.

Mo gripped my arm. Her anticipation was an aberration that repulsed me. Something terrible was happening outside, yet Mo looked upon it like a sacred revelation. I wanted to look away, but I couldn't.

The rabbit's body lit with a shower of luminescence. I could almost see the molecules rearranging themselves, changing composition. Its fur dissolved into its body and its paws melted away. The ears ran in rivulets down a head that no longer had eyes or a nose. Everything lost definition until there was nothing left but a smooth, glowing blob, held together with fragile skin.

The thing that had been a rabbit burst like a viscous bubble and drained into the barren soil, seeking the depths of the earth with a purpose, as if rushing to catch up with fellow rabbits already there.

Mo exhaled a joyous sigh.

I looked at her, horror rising within me. Around her eyes, just underneath the lids, silver light burned.

* * *

We are taught that it took billions of years for life to grow and evolve on earth. Within two weeks of the collision, total extinction barreled forward at a speed that left little time for anything, even panic.

Indeed, those that were inclined to panic were in the minority. I wondered if I was the only one. The rest of humanity seemed to embrace the same baffling rapture as Mo.

Television networks showed masses of people all over the world standing in open, barren areas, waiting for the first quarter moon to rise. With arms outstretched toward the brightness, they smiled and sang as their blood ran silver and their limbs melted into their bodies. Their faces dripped down their necks and, within an hour, what had been physical humans were gone, drained into the earth, leaving only inert clothing and jewelry behind. The correspondents that were left reported that the "metamorphoses" had reached the five billion mark. Wheat fields and grasslands were gone, they said, and forests were reduced to a few stunted trees that would probably disappear within a day. Almost all animals were gone, and even the fish in the sea were melting into the waves.

There was no shortage of pundits. Organized religions of every denomination announced that God had had enough of this iniquitous world and this was His final punishment. Some claimed it was some sort of death ray from an advanced and evidently hostile alien race. And still others claimed it was a natural event, a random cosmic cleansing for which earth had, somehow, drawn the short straw.

I couldn't see how any explanation mattered. This was the end, a concept my rational mind could not digest, yet floated with sick certainty deep within. My preprogrammed brain tried to make plans for a future that didn't exist, and each renewed realization of this futility was a gut punch that left me gasping for breath.

* * *

Mo's hair was gone, and her skin had taken on a smooth, thin texture that looked like it would split at the slightest contact. In the dark, silver light oozed from her pores, bathing her in augural effulgence.

I had the same glow underneath my fingernails. With every breath the lunar light tingled in my lungs. I avoided the mirror. I didn't want to see the moon behind my eyes.

But where I felt nauseating dread, Mo was joyous. She smiled, and moonlight shone from behind her teeth.

"Accept it," she told me. "Release your heart from this world. Allow yourself the beauty of the call."

I shivered.

* * *

Outside, nothing moved. Even in daylight, the stillness was broken only by the friction of the wind against something dead, like our house. I wondered if Mo and I were the only two people left on earth. I did not dare get in my car and drive around. I didn't want to see nothing but barrenness, a hollowed-out land in place of what I used to call home.

The moon built within me. It seared through my veins as my heart pounded it to every capillary, every cell. It was a thing alive under my skin, a sentience that pulled at me to go outside into the night, rewarding this thought with chills of rapture that left me nearly mindless.

I fought the inevitability of my acquiescence, and the maddening throes of alien ecstasy that came with it.

I felt the call, as Mo named it, and in the silver that sang through every nerve, in the liquid light that illuminated every cell, I understood its purpose. The essence of every living thing, from microbes and bacteria to plants and animals and humans was assuming a singular identity, to assimilate with the energy of the earth. The planet and the life it had spawned were becoming one, a transcendence of awareness, an expansion of knowledge growing toward omniscience.

Nascent godhood.

I couldn't fight this for much longer. But while I could, I did. The obsolescence of individuality was anathema to me, and I wondered why so many others, including Mo, were so eager for it.

Mo could no longer move under her own power. Her fingers and toes had dripped away. I think she was holding on merely to see my acceptance. My old human mind insisted I was going to lose her. But that wasn't true. We would be one, with everyone and everything else.

I didn't know which was worse.

* * *

It was over.

The full moon shone through our windows, but it didn't touch the corner where I held Mo. It didn't need to. The luminescence of our bodies was enough.

Mo's eyes were bright and featureless. Thick silver veins snaked underneath her skin. Her breathing was ragged, and her body was soft and formless. Everything within was liquefying. I had mere minutes left with her.

She asked me to bring her outside. Finally, I gave in to the inevitable. I could not refuse her.

Although she weighed no more than before, I struggled to lift her. My muscles and bones were softening. But I would honor her wish. These were our last moments within our old forms, and I would do anything Mo wanted for as long as I was able.

No stars were visible in the moonlit sky. I carried Mo to the center of the barren yard and laid her down, then sat beside her. The direct moonlight quickened the process within me; my body settled like butter left in the heat.

Mo's clothing deflated as her body lost its form and seeped away. She never lost her smile.

"Don't be afraid, Gary."

Her face smoothed over, becoming a silver oval. The skin of her body ruptured, and she gushed into the earth. Mo's clothes settled into emptiness.

I looked at the moon, and, finally, all fear left me. There was no pain as my body liquefied and trickled away. The silver-white orb bathed me with a gentle light, encouraging me, and then fading as what had been my body broke and soaked into the ground. I raced downward between rock and particles of soil. The multitudes of others awaited me, assimilated me, and my consciousness was absorbed as part of a beauteous whole.

We joined our will with the earth, and new life was born. Single-celled creatures populated the seas and green shoots sprouted from the ground.

Nothing would be as it had been. The old way hadn't worked. The same mistake would not be made again.

Ponytail Protest

Jill Fague

My mother had many talents. Styling hair was not one of them. Most of the time, I accepted a half ponytail secured by an elastic with two plastic gumballs atop my head. My mom, obviously challenged by her fine motor skills, could manage the task, and my little tomboy self favored this style. Nothing fancy, but stubborn strands brushed away from my face, suitable for a day of chasing my brother and cousins. More accurately, I would likely find myself running from my brother's assassination attempts. Those I could handle, but school picture day sentenced me to a childhood filled with psychological issues.

Nope, no half ponytail allowed for the yearly tradition that tortured my soul. For some reason, my mother always insisted I wear my hair down for elementary school pictures. She left me no choice. Before the bus arrived, she would attack my scalp with a scorching-hot curling iron. Defenseless, I could only squirm and complain until she finished. The result? Dirty blonde curls sticking out disastrously from the sides of my head.

My self-esteem sank to the shallows, mirroring the pitiful doll from *Island of the Misfit Toys*. I guess it could have been worse, like the poor girl whose mom must have been drunk each year on picture day. *But how was it possible? My mom curled her own hair and set it every day of her life, yet she caused a train wreck with mine. Did she have two left hands? Was she blind?*

One summer morning, I woke up in the screen house in our backyard. (I had begged my parents to sleep outside the previous evening.) It's safe to say I enjoyed getting my own way. Of course, I immediately went in search of my mom so she could fix my hair. She was not in the house, and her car was missing from the driveway. At least my older brother, Michael, was still in bed, which meant a temporary reprieve from bow and arrow attacks or Chinese stars of doom.

My childhood was like a perpetual game of Manhunt, and my brother had all the weapons. Besides a bow and arrow and ninja stars, his arsenal included a BB gun, slingshots, even chestnuts on the end of a string. Somehow, I became his prey. So, I ran. I ran for my life.

I ran from my mother, too. Only she chased me with a fly swatter, and boy, does it sting when you get whacked on bare calves with a plastic fly swatter. I almost preferred getting hit with BBs. I had to be quick if I wanted to survive, and I always put up a good fight.

Relieved that Michael was still sleeping, I checked on Erin, my little sister. She was also fast asleep. I figured my mother couldn't have gone too far without her. I grabbed a brush from the bathroom, bolted through the house, and let the screen door slam behind me. Jumping down the cement steps in my bare feet, I ran across our yard over to my grandparents' house next door. Mom was not over there either.

"Hey Nana, where's my mom?"

"She went next door. They are protesting today," my grandmother told me.

Ugh, I should have known. Now I would have to face a bunch of people if I wanted my ponytail.

Then Nana warned me, "She said to stay in your own yard until she comes back. And keep away from that road!"

Have you met me? Did I ever cooperate? I mean, I was the legendary grandchild who spit at my nana after she threw me out of her house for being fresh earlier that summer. Of course, that brilliant action incited my aunt's wrath, and as she tried to shove me out of the breezeway, my canvas sneaker got stuck in the sliding screen door. I wrenched my foot out of it, fully intending to abandon it and run for my life. But not so fast. Auntie snatched up my traitorous footwear, wrestled me into a crude headlock, and repeatedly whacked me on the head with it as she dragged me back into my own yard. Of course, I kicked and screamed as if my aunt were a homicidal maniac trying to haul me into a white van. The nerve. Nana didn't even save me from my aunt's evil clutches. *Like I was going to listen to her now.*

In a huff, I exited my nana's house. Naturally, I turned right, toward my neighbors' house, instead of heading back into my own yard as directed. I needed to find my mother: Mission Ponytail.

We lived on a twisty, narrow, tree-lined road with a pond directly across from our farmhouse. It was a pretty, quiet backdrop until the menacing eighteen-wheeled tractor trailer trucks began barreling past our house several times a day, dumping tires and other hazardous waste across acres of privately-owned landfill property. The situation quickly became an environmental nightmare. Sometimes I imagined terrifying lagoon creatures, spawned from toxic sludge, roaming our neighborhood under the cover of darkness.

Trips to the town council meetings and community outcry did nothing to help our neighborhood. The trucks kept rolling. Not only did my mother fear one of her children getting run over, she feared the contamination of our water supply, and she feared the deranged man who owned the dump. He had threatened her and our entire family more than once after my mom's community action put his business smack into the DEM spotlight.

At one point, according to *The New York Times* archive, "Federal environmental agents, fended off with threats of gunfire, said they would no longer venture onto his land without an armed escort." Apparently, my mother wasn't the only target in the crosshairs of this backwoods bully. She even learned how to shoot a handgun after one of his more colorful tirades. My father seemed about ready to stuff that guy's filthy, ever-present cigar right down his obnoxious throat. I just hoped he would light it first.

I stomped my way across my grandparents' lawn and into my neighbors' yard on the opposite side. *Honestly, why did it have to be so difficult? I just needed my mom to do my hair. Priorities, people!* Brush in hand, I scanned the crowd for my mother. I expected to see the usual: cars parked on the side of the road (making it tricky, if not impassible, for the tractor trailers), neighbors chatting, and possibly a small crowd. Though, on this morning, the protest had reached a new level. My neighbors and my mother had endured enough.

Tiptoeing through the wet grass, searching the crowd, my brain processed the eighteen-wheeler stopped in the middle of our serpentine road. Stuck. The only way it could continue would be *over* the cars parked on the edge of the road. Barring any sort of magic spell, that was unlikely.

But I did not see my mom among the familiar faces. *Where the heck was she? Why couldn't she just brush my hair before saving the world?*

Then I spotted her.

She was lying in the road! A human speed bump. *What was she thinking?* I obviously knew my mother liked getting her own way (stubbornness ran deep in my DNA), but this was madness. *What if they ran her over? What if that crazy guy from the dump really tried to kill her? My dad would never be able to scoop my hair into a ponytail of any kind. C'mon, Mom!*

Mortified by both my appearance and my mother's behavior, I stood off to the side of the commotion, keeping my rat's nest hair hidden. Sadly, my embarrassment had not reached maximum capacity.

Then the cops came.

Seriously? Were they arresting my mom? Forsaken, I watched as an officer picked my mother up from the pavement, walked her toward the side of the road, and secured her in handcuffs. *Was that necessary? Did she look like a bloodthirsty soccer mom or something?* Like the cops on TV, he placed his hand on the top of her head and guided her into the back seat of his cruiser. With some degree of satisfaction, I realized my mom wouldn't like that. No one touched her hair after she had set it for the day. *Humph, at least someone got her hair done. Must be nice.*

The cruiser window was rolled half-down, so my mom launched her car keys out of the opening. As they sailed through the air, landing on our neighbor's lawn, my mom shouted, "Someone take care of my kids!" I cringed at her emotional outburst.

I'm guessing my father was at work that day, or perhaps my mother just didn't think he was up to the task of watching his own kids. Truth be told, my father may have needed backup to get through an entire day with the three of us. After all, we did have Michael to consider, and Erin couldn't yet fend for herself in the event of a brotherly ninja attack. At least she slept through the whole humiliating incident.

Although my mother's shout seemed melodramatic, she had been arrested in front of the entire neighborhood. Cuffed and stuffed.

Throwing my brush, I stood pouting with tangled hair hanging in my reddened face. I could protest too.

Waking Up

Theresa Schimmel

Will awakes first. The slow steady rhythm of Kyoko's breath warms his chest. Lifting thick strands of black hair from her face, he kisses her tenderly on the forehead. Her eyes flicker. She clutches the sheet and turns over for another hour of sleep.

He pulls on jeans and walks barefoot to the kitchen. Three years of the nine-to-five working world has created autopilot. Reaching for the coffeepot, he scoops the grounds, pours the water, and plugs in the machine. The aroma will rouse her. She needs the usual two-and-a-half cups to get moving. Turning the shower on, he brushes his teeth while waiting for the water to heat. They want to get there early before the crowd, so he forgoes shaving, steps into the tub, and lathers his underarms. Watching steam rise to the ceiling, he takes a deep breath as the memories of a year ago come flooding back. It began with the phone ringing as he rushed out the door.

"Will, it's Blake. Have you calculated those figures for Universal Life?"

"Almost done, sir."

"The meeting's at our old office at the Trade Center at nine. Jackson's coming with me. His figures are done. I'd hoped to take you, but since you've got work to do, it will have to wait. Have them done today, Will. I'll check in with you when I get back."

"Will do. See you in the office." Shit. He'd completed the 2002 financial projections, but the insurance company had requested a spreadsheet model with a two-year projection. He never got to it last night. Instead, he talked to Kyoko for hours and then worked on his latest composition, finally crashing at three in the morning. Will passed the latest actuary test, but he knew if he was going to make it in the company he'd have to put in more late hours. Blake said as much at lunch last week.

"Will, you've got one of the brightest minds in the company. Your test scores show that, your work shows that. But it takes more if you want to be promoted. Everyone has to pay their dues, Will. Burn the midnight oil, show that you're passionate about where this company is headed. Can you do that?

"Yes, sir. I've always loved working with numbers."

"Takes more than math ability. You need to put your heart and soul into the company. I've brought more clients in than any manager before me. That meant a little more legwork than anyone else. You want to move up, don't you, Will?

"Uh, of course."

"Then take my advice. The company will be good to you if you're good to it."

Last night his briefcase sat unopened in the living room while he composed. The composition was getting closer to what he wanted. He is constantly revising, creating a conversation between dramatic piano chords and the sweet clear tones of flute, clarinet, and cello. Kyoko understands his passion for composing; she thinks he should quit his job and go back to college for his doctorate in music. But he has lots of time for that. Life now is about friends, parties, and trendy bars in the Big Apple. In another year he might make enough money to move from Brooklyn to Manhattan. To do that, he'd have to take Blake's advice. Pull out that briefcase every night instead of sitting at his keyboard. If he'd done that last night, Blake would be taking him, instead of Jackson, to the World Trade Center meeting today.

Where would Kyoko be in 2002? She'd receive her graduate degree from the Rhode Island School of Design. Then what? Kyoko. He is afraid to name his feelings for her. She'd come into his life unexpectedly. He wasn't looking for a serious relationship. But the thought of losing her scares him. Their last phone conversation was one of the few times she spoke of the future.

"My portfolio is really coming along. Professor Williams thinks I should feature my tapestry work. Says it has a very unique style. Did I tell you that I've been given the technical assistant job for his class this spring?"

"No. That's great, Kyoko! Should put a little more money in your pocket. Maybe we can plan spring break together - someplace exotic!"

He heard her deep-throated laugh on the phone. "Will, I'm not just doing it for the money."

"I know. I know. It'll add to your résumé. But the money is always nice. Where do you think we should go? I've got two weeks' vacation saved up."

"I'd like to spend that time with you, Will, but I hope to go to Japan this spring."

He bites his lip, letting the phone slip from his ear.

"Will, did you hear me?"

"Yes. You're going to Japan."

"My grandparents are starting to have health problems. I don't think I should put it off."

"I understand."

"Also, my uncle is arranging an interview for me at Nezu Institute of Fine Arts."

"In Japan?"

"Of course, in Japan, silly."

"I didn't know you had plans to return to Japan. Last I knew you were going to apply for jobs here in the States."

"Well, yes, but they will be harder to get, I'm sure, and my uncle knows the Nezu curator who told him there will be an opening. You know how hard I've worked. This could be my chance, jump start my career."

Will clenches his jaw, unsure what to say. Japan? He didn't want her thousands of miles away. Didn't their relationship mean more than that?

"Will, are you still there?"

"Ah, yes, just picking up some of my sheet music that fell on the floor."

"Thanks for sending me that CD of your latest piece. I loved it, especially the ending. Have you sent it to anyone else? How about Professor Miangi? He was such a fan of your work when you were at Brown. Did I tell you I saw him the other day in the cafeteria? I was surprised he remembered me as we had only met that one time. But he immediately said hello and asked about you. I told him that you were working as an actuary in New York. He shook his head and said that he wishes you would apply for the doctoral program in composition. He thinks you'd get accepted easily. I think you should too, Will."

"Someday, maybe." He didn't want to have this conversation again. She couldn't understand why he wanted to stay in New York, when his true passion was composing. But he'd never make much money doing that, would he? He'd already received two raises, and if he passed the next actuary test, he'd be making three figures. And then there was the nightlife. There was no other place like New York City for nightlife. Since dating Kyoko, however, his weekend routine had changed. Friday nights he still made the rounds with friends, but the remainder of his weekends was spent with Kyoko.

Last Saturday, instead of going to the Latitude for billiards and beer with the guys, he picked up Kyoko at the train station and suggested they go to the 21 Club. He was anxious to show her the posh lounge, order from the extensive menu, and sit under the dazzling chandeliers. She declined, saying it was much too expensive. Instead, they went to Elia's Greek restaurant on Third Avenue. He was at least partially successful in expanding her limited cuisine. After five years in the States, she still ate mostly Asian food. He remembered how her eyes lit up as she tasted baklava for the first time, licking every drop of the sugary syrup, and then ordering a second one to eat on the way to the play. She chose to see the off-Broadway play Topdog/Under-dog and insisted on paying for her own ticket.

After the play, they ran in the rain to a nearby coffee shop. The dé-cor was classic old-style diner, with red barstools at the counter, laminate tabletops, and vinyl booths. They slid into one and ordered two coffees and a cheesecake to share. Kyoko analyzed the two brothers in the play as the waitress poured coffee. She added two sugar packets and set the spoon on the saucer, spilling some coffee on the I Love New York plastic placemat.

He took a napkin from the dispenser to wipe the brown puddle off the noted landmarks and 2001 calendar. As their fingers touched, the con-versation paused briefly before she asked, "What are you thinking, Will?"

He hesitated. He was thinking of her, of next year, and the year after that.

"That I agree with your analysis. The younger brother was manipu-lative, but it was a defense mechanism."

She smiled. "I wasn't sure you were listening. I can always tell when you're distracted. Your fingers start tapping."

How did she know him so well? He reached over and wiped the crumbs from the corner of her mouth. He had told her once that she was rather messy for a Japanese girl. She then chided him for his stereotypical comment. She was right, of course. It was silly of him to make such gener-alizations. While there were many Asian students at Brown, especially in the performing arts department, he had only come to know Hana, a fourth-year cello major. They were practicing his cello étude piece at her apart-ment, when he met Kyoko, Hana's roommate.

His first impression was not a positive one. The door slammed, an-nouncing Kyoko's arrival and interrupting practice. It was hard to see her at first. With a tote bag over one shoulder, a backpack slung over the other, and books cradled in her arms, only two ebony eyes were visible. Within minutes, the living room was full of bolts of cloth and opened books. Hana explained that Kyoko was a Rhode Island School of Design student, im-mersed in creating a tapestry mural. After brief introductions, Kyoko com-mandeered the kitchen table to spread her design plans. She never looked up. He was not accustomed to being so intensely ignored.

It wasn't until his third visit to Hana's that he actually spoke with Kyoko. She opened the door for him. "I'm sorry. Hana called to say that she'll be late. She hoped that you'd wait for her. Do you want a cup of cof-fee? I was just about to have one."

"Sure. Make it black, please."

"My father drinks it black, too. I can't seem to give up the sugar."

"I thought Japanese drank tea."

She laughed. It was deep and throaty. He thought it sexy. "I drink tea sometimes, but my father got me turned on to coffee as a teenager, and I'm hooked. I can offer you some rice cakes to go with it, though. Will that be Japanese enough for you?" Looking across the table in the dimly lit diner and recalling that first cup of coffee together six months ago, he realized that he never wanted the conversation with Kyoko to end.

Back at his apartment, they'd made love. His hand fit perfectly in the small of her back and he relished the slight shiver of her spine as his fingers trailed. In the morning, they curled up on the couch to watch Sponge-Bob, laughing like schoolchildren while crunching toasted bagels. As she licked the marmalade off the top of the bagel, she begged him to spend the day with her. Guiltily, he called in sick, even though Mondays were the busiest at the office.

She left early Tuesday morning on the train to Providence. As they sat in Penn Station, she leaned against his shoulder and wound her fingers through his. He glanced at the station clock, aware that he'd be late but not wanting to give up even one minute with Kyoko. The train pulled in exactly at eight. He lifted her suitcase and waved goodbye, then watched as she walked through the train, settled into a window seat, and tucked her hand-sewn quilted jacket of silver and mauve under her cheek as a pillow.

Will turns the shower off, and pushes those memories aside as the glass door opens. In the fogged bathroom he sees Kyoko's small feet on the tiled floor. She offers him a cup of coffee, then yawns. "Do you want a bagel?"

"Do we have time to eat?"

"I'll put them in a bag, and we can eat them on the subway." They dress quickly, gulp their coffee, and grab the bagels before heading out the door. The apartment elevator rises slowly. Will taps his foot in the hallway. "Let's take the stairs." As they descend to the street and walk toward the subway, he is flooded with the memory of that day, a year ago, after he put Kyoko on the train, taking this very same walk. The morning began pleasantly enough – but then…the nightmarish images return. His heart starts to race. Beads of sweat form on his hairline. The present fades into the past and he is there once again. ….

The last two blocks before the subway entrance take Will past Prospect Park. Shading his eyes from the glare of the morning sun, he looks upward. The clear flute-like melody of a Carolina wren punctuates the urban din. Kyoko would often tease him about his birding, how he would stop mid-stride when hearing a birdcall, searching for its source. For his birthday she

15

had given him a bird book. Thoughtful but practical Kyoko. He would not see her for another week.

He scrambles down the subway stairwell. The jostling begins as he pushes his way through the door and quickly grabs a bar before the doors close. Wafts of Starbucks and after-shave mingle with stale urine and grease. Newspapers snap open, laptops unfold, eyelids droop. The early morning commute is a forty-minute ride with no eye contact or conversation. Even with his feet planted on the sticky subway floor, his body sways. The next stop is Bergen Street. After three years, he knows every line and station. Moving from their World Trade Office to New Jersey two months ago added ten minutes to his commute. He misses working at the twin towers, when he would walk out into the courtyard, surrounded by the great steel beams and marvel at the 110 floors rising above him.

The subway is now above ground. Three more stops before arriving at the World Trade Center. He catches a whiff of smoke. Will peers through the glass windows and sees a gray mass. Some kind of emergency, sure to delay his arrival. He acts on impulse and gets off at Jay Street to make a different connection for the PATH train to New Jersey. Arriving at work, his head is filled with thoughts of Kyoko. There had been no discussions of commitment or their future. At twenty-six, he has lots of time. No need for a precipitous decision.

The elevator doors open and he strides into the twentieth-floor office. From the expansive picture window, he looks across the river to the World Trade Center and gasps. A cavernous hole gouges the North Tower. Dark gray smoke, like an immense storm cloud, envelops the top floors. Then, from the corner of his eye, he sees it, a plane speeding directly toward the South Tower. Within seconds, it strikes, causing an immediate fireball three-fourths of the way up the 110 floors. The meeting – with Blake and Jackson. It was on the 94th floor. His knees buckle.

At 9:35, Will takes the last PATH train into Manhattan after the attack. No longer are the passengers sheathed in their commuter cocoons. His legs press against two teenage girls. He looks down and sees a pimple-ridden face with two pools of watery blue eyes staring past him. The girl hiccups repeatedly, ignoring the whimpering of her friend. He smells the sweat of the man across from him - dressed in a business suit, his face bloated and ashen, who frantically punches numbers into a cell phone. There is a faint smell of vomit. At the back of the train, a woman holds her child as he retches into a paper bag. Will holds tight to the bar.

The car doors open. People spill out, bounding up the stairs. Despite the surge, he stops and stares upward. A young woman pushes against him, sobbing, "My husband works there. I . . ." Her voice chokes as she leans against him. Instinctively, he wraps one arm around her shoulder. The moisture of her tears seep through his dress white shirt, while mascara runs down her cheeks. He stares at the black smudges. A violent explosion tears them apart. Will looks up. The South Tower is missing an entire floor. Fire and smoke envelop the two pillars.

He shudders when he sees them. From high above, they jump. First a man, his dark sports coat billowing out like mini-wings, shirt and tie flapping. Next, a woman, her body tumbling, as in a circus act. He turns, afraid to see or hear the impact. A horrified cry erupts from the masses as the entire South Tower collapses. Soot and gray ash roll toward him as bodies crash into each other like erratic pinballs. He hears panicked screams as they push onward. Will trips over some broken glass and falls to the pavement; a foot crushes his hand. Quickly, he scrambles to his feet and glances at his cracked wristwatch: 9:59.

Escape. He looks for the closest subway. They have shut down. Hundreds press by him, heading toward the Brooklyn Bridge. His head throbbing, he pictures them, more planes coming. How many will come? From where? He mouths Kyoko's name.

Should he follow the crowd across the Brooklyn Bridge? Or will that be the next target? He maps an alternative route. He will walk uptown a few more blocks and take the Manhattan Bridge toward Brooklyn. Past City Hall Park, on to St. James Place and then Chatham Square. That would bring him into Chinatown, where he could get onto Canal Street, leading on to the Manhattan Bridge. He knows it will take hours.

He licks the blood dripping from the palm of his hand. A sea of gray ghosts trudge past him. He looks into the eyes of each one. A communion of lost souls. He thinks of Dante's Inferno, and strains of Liszt's Dante's Symphony play in his head. The Descent theme with its chromatic line of sharps and flats to match the inscription over the gates of Hell: Abandon all hope, ye who enter here. Despite the heat, Will shivers. He walks all day hearing sirens in the distance.

At 5:43 that afternoon, Will opens his apartment door, and collapses on the floor. His body shakes, and he cannot make it stop. Head throbbing, he realizes he hasn't eaten all day. He sticks his face under the kitchen sink, gulping water from the running faucet. Tearing into the bread bag, he mechanically chews three slices. A ringing sound. Must be the echo of sirens. The answering machine clicks in. "Will, it's Kyoko. Please, please be there." He picks up the phone.

"Kyoko. I'm here." She sobs. It is the first time he's heard her cry, and his voice chokes.

It is the sound of her voice on the street calling to him that brings him back. "Will, are you okay?" He looks down. Kyoko is frowning, shaking his arm. "You scared me. I … you seemed so far away. You were having another flashback, weren't you?"

He nods.

"We don't have to do this, Will."

He takes a few deep breaths before reaching for Kyoko's hand, hoping her touch will still the shaking. "No, I want to. Let's go."

Brooklyn's streets are almost deserted as they walk to the subway. They pass Dashi Market, where Kyoko buys her miso sauce, ao-nori, and other Asian ingredients. Calm returns with the repetitive clicking of Kyoko's heels on the pavement. He realizes that she is half-running to keep up with his long legs. He likes her diminutiveness, the way he can hold both her hands in his one; curl her body in his lap. Gingerly, they step onto the subway. It too is almost abandoned. Will squints as the sun pours through the scratched glass subway windows.

They exit at Battery Park, where seagulls perch on the posts bordering the harbor. Will notes the brilliance of the September sunshine, the clarity of the blue sky, identical to a year ago. Early morning joggers dart past them. Hand in hand, Will and Kyoko approach the Koenig Sphere, formerly located at the World Trade Center Plaza as a monument to world peace. Will recalls its brassy gleam atop the granite fountain where office workers would sit eating lunch and watch glistening water shower the sphere's base. Now, the sphere sits upright on the Eisenhower Mall in Battery Park, fringed with newly planted poplars and park benches. While still structurally intact, a deep gash runs through its fifteen foot diameter. It stands defiant, wearing its war-inflicted scar.

For a long time they stand beneath the gold orb. Squeezing Kyoko's hand, Will's wedding band touches hers. She leans into him, and he kisses the top of her head. Together they turn and head back to the subway station. They forgo the memorial ceremonies. Will does not need speeches to remember. Besides, today would be a day of packing as they prepare for the move. Will's university classes begin in four days. Their new Providence apartment is waiting for them.

An Evening Babysitting

by Pamela Carey

Charley and I maneuvered Dylan and Scottie, the ten-month-old twins, into their highchairs and buckled them in. No accidents on our watch! The boys reminded me of baby birds, with their necks thrown back, their mouths open, and wails coming from deep in their throats. We began to shovel baby food in, as fast as possible.

Around this time, our son and daughter-in-law attempted their exit for a pleasant evening out. Our three-year-old granddaughter, Olivia, jumped down from her chair at the kitchen table and clung to her mother's legs. "Me too! Me too!" she wailed.

Our daughter-in-law placed Olivia back in front of her mac and cheese and applesauce. A fixed smile never left her face. "We'll be home right after we eat, Liv, and we'll come in to kiss you good night." Julie planted a smack on her daughter's lips.

Tom and Julie hustled through the laundry room, locking the door to the garage behind them. Olivia followed into the laundry room. Her screams began to grow in intensity and pitch when she heard their car turn over. Her brothers tried to outdo her. Three of them were now in falsetto. Unable to budge the locked outer door, Olivia threw herself onto the laundry room floor in the dark and sobbed. I went in to hug her.

"Come on, Liv, come finish your supper. Granny and Papa are here and your brothers want to eat with you. Mommy and Daddy will be home right after they eat."

"No! Go away, Granny!" she screamed, pushing me when I tried to pick her up.

"Okay, you stay here till you get hungry."

I resumed my place in front of Dylan and Scottie and continued shoveling. Both boys attempted to grab their little spoons, to guide the food in faster. When they had finished, orange and green mush was up their nostrils, down their necks, in their hair, and on their eyelids. Charley and I alternated hosing them down over the kitchen sink and hosing ourselves down. The wailing continued from the laundry room.

Deposited on the floor, Dylan reached the laundry room door just before Olivia slammed it shut. He began banging with his palm, concerned for his sister. "Go away!" was the response.

"Liv, why not come out for an ice cream sandwich?" I propositioned. Anything to stop the wailing! It took ten minutes, but the ploy worked. A blubbery, red-faced miss peered around the door and ran to my knees for a hug.

I picked her up and cuddled her hard. Snot draped over my shoulder and neck. "Can I have ice cream now?"

"I think this would be an excellent time for ice cream," I told her, stroking her head. So much for balanced nutrition! The mac and cheese was like cement, anyway. Charley dumped Liv's dinner down the disposal and I reached for a vanilla ice cream sandwich.

After her "dinner," Olivia went to paint in the family room. Scottie was under a tablecloth, connecting oversized plastic blocks in his "clubhouse." Dylan began pulling himself up against the coffee table.

There was a rubber protector around the perimeter of the table, but one corner protruded where the boys had pulled the rubber off. Dylan got halfway up and toppled over. Of course, he fell onto the unprotected corner and began screaming.

"Oh, Lord! Not an accident already! They just left!" I couldn't believe it. Charley cuddled Dylan, calmed him down, and examined the eye. It was beginning to swell, but at least the skin wasn't broken. I ran for some ice to wrap in a wet towel, but that exercise was futile with a toddler. He whimpered and pushed the cold pack away. Scottie peered out from under the tablecloth and resumed building.

"He'll have a shiner in the morning!" Charley predicted.

Then I smelled something foul.

"That didn't take long! Charley, do you smell something?"

"I don't smell anything!"

"Yeah, I'll bet!" I leaned over Dylan's behind and turned away. My eyes were watering.

"Mother of God!" I held Dylan at arm's length. "Charley, undo the gate while I hold him!" After Charley hit the release button, I ran up the stairs with Dylan's bottom facing upward and plopped him on the changing table. I grabbed two ankles and lifted. Green slime ran up his back and down to his knees. I pressed one foot on the lever to open the trash bucket and attempted to throw the used diaper inside when Dylan began to squirm. Not just squirm, but roll over to grab the tube of ointment next to him. "Shit!" I mumbled, as I looked at my green forearm and changing table cover. Then I burst out laughing, realizing what I'd said. That made Dylan pause long enough so I could take a couple of swipes at his bottom. "Into the tub for you, buster!"

Under the lukewarm stream from the faucet, I held him tight with one hand beneath his armpit, while my other hand used the washcloth on his moldy-looking bottom.

A piercing scream suspended my rub-a-dub. I heard Charley running. In one motion, I grabbed a towel and brought Dylan out of the tub. He and I ran down the stairs toward the scream, water dripping over the newly refinished floors. Then I got to the gate at the bottom. Childproof? How about adultproof? I yanked to disengage the release button, and the contraption crashed to the floor. I charged down the last two steps, stepped around the gate, and put Dylan, still wrapped in his towel, down. Before I could pick him up again I had to reposition the gate, in case the other guy came crawling out to investigate.

Charley was already kneeling on the side of the toilet, cuddling Olivia. She had nothing on from the waist down. Blood dripped on the tile floor, obviously from a split lip. Depositing Dylan on the floor next to Charley, I closed the door behind me and made a beeline back to the freezer for another icepack.

No sign of Scottie. When I got back to the accident scene, Dylan had begun finger-painting in his sister's blood. I scooped him up again.

"I found her on the floor in front of the toilet," Charley said. "She must have fallen off."

As he held her against his chest, Olivia's screaming subsided. "Did you have to poop?" he asked her.

An affirmative nod.

"Did you fall over?" Liv nestled into his chest, snot covering his shirt. She pointed at the metal wastebasket.

"Did you fall onto the wastebasket?" he pursued. Again, she nodded affirmatively. It looked like a MASH unit in the bathroom - blood on the floor, a black eye that continued to swell, and a puffy, cut lip.

I deposited Dylan, naked as a newborn, with Scottie in the "clubhouse" under the tablecloth. Then I cleaned the bathroom floor with paper towels, while Charley held the cold pack to Olivia's lip. She was on the toilet, trying to resume her business. She pushed Charley's arm away, as her brother had.

I returned to the family room. Dylan was still in the "clubhouse," but Scottie was standing at his sister's easel with a silly grin on his face. Suspicious, I went over to have a look. On the floor was a plastic cup with paint sediment at the bottom. The paintbrush lay nearby, while ochre-colored liquid seeped into the Oriental carpet a couple of feet away. "Oh God!" I wondered how many times I would call on the Almighty that evening. Olivia had left her paints in the toddler zone when she went to the bathroom.

I encircled Scottie and lifted him, and together we headed for a clean cloth and a bottle of carpet shampoo from the laundry room. Scottie teetered on my knee as I sprayed and scrubbed. Back and forth, up and down, back and forth, Scottie swayed with my strokes. My L4 disc must have relocated – my back was killing me!

Just then, Dylan crawled around the corner of the sofa, still naked. "I forgot about you, Dylan! Hope you didn't pee anywhere!" There was no evidence of moisture under the table. "I think it's everyone's bedtime! Let's each pick a book and we'll read in Liv's room."

Charley got the twins into their superhero pajamas while Olivia retrieved her pink nightgown with the tutu from her dresser. All three kids sandwiched into Olivia's queen-sized bed with me in the middle. Charley sat in a chair, his eyelids drooping.

After three skinny books which Olivia had memorized so I couldn't skip pages, I said, "It's time for sleep now. We love you and we'll see you in the morning." I kissed the fat lip, the swollen eye, and Scottie's cheek. Charley did the same, tucking in the twins. I turned off Olivia's overhead light, made sure the nightlight was plugged in, and closed her door. Next stop was the changing table. I unzipped the cover and replaced it with a clean one. We heard a crib banging against the wall in Scottie's room, but disregarded it and went downstairs to clean up any remaining evidence. I deposited the changing table cover in the washer. Dinner? We were too tired to eat.

At 8 p.m. we flopped onto the guest room bed in our clothes. I couldn't move. My L4 disc was killing me from picking up the twins. It would take twenty minutes for the pain reliever to kick in. I was downing those things like they were another food group! I began to reconstruct what had happened between 6 and 8 p.m. - a temper tantrum, a black eye, a split lip, paint spilled onto the Oriental carpet, baby food in my hair, and green poop up my arm!

So much for nothing happening on our watch! What's wrong with playpens, anyway? Do young parents think it will stifle the kids' curiosity to play within a three-foot radius instead of 1200 feet? Our kids turned out okay, didn't they? They grew up with imaginations and clear, rational thinking. A playpen made them stay focused, that's the difference! We didn't give in if they cried a little. Parents are afraid to say 'No!' today. They want to be their kids' best friends. Charley and I weren't afraid to say 'No,' but I did put him in the role of disciplinarian most of the time. I know he didn't appreciate that.

And this whole time-out baloney is exactly that – baloney! Our boys weren't psychologically damaged when we gave them a little thump on the behind. Olivia sits on a time-out chair in a corner and turns around and sings to us. Then her parents move the chair and she peels the wallpaper off the wall. By then, everyone is so upset they forgot what the punishment was for.

And I never cooked a separate meal for our kids. Why did Livia have to eat mac and cheese when I'd already made pasta and chicken?

And I don't understand why they take Olivia in bed with them when she wakes up during the night. The twins I can understand – they're only ten months and it's a process of elimination to find out why they're crying. But Livia can tell them. Why don't they just lie with her for a while, then go back to their own bed?

Do I hear someone crying? It sounds like Liv!

"It's all right, honey. Come sleep with Granny and Papa for a while."

The Memory Keeper

Debbie Kaiman Tillinghast

My memories live in a wooden box,
Tucked between grayed cards
Long flecked with stains of lard
And crumbs of sticky Snickerdoodles.
They wait in silence,
Nestled in the corner, packed in tight
Until I lift the lid and free them to take flight.
They wander through the cupboards of my mind,
Faded words precisely written,
Some dimmed beyond recognition
Others holding hands with yesterday
Drawing faces in the air, as they float across the kitchen.
A hologram sits in the waiting chair,
Wrinkled hands reach out to guide
The tiny ones that hold a rolling pin,
And I tell her where I've been.

Cookies marked with raisins to form a monkey's face,
The kitchen door bursts open
Spilling cold and children into stove-warmed space.
Gentle voices whisper as I hold the wooden box
Vibrating with stories my ears alone can hear,
Though not clearly seen they shimmer for me there.
Memories cling together in one delicious spot,
I close the lid to keep them safe,
Discard them? I cannot.

Mother Goose and His Goslings

Dean Fachon

On the edge of a salt marsh along the lower arm of Cape Cod, there's a place where time almost stood still. Several decades ago, before rampant development began scarring the Cape, the marsh was declared a "wildlife sanctuary," and building ceased with no more than a few houses salted along a dirt and gravel road. An idyllic location, it was would-be prime property were it not for the Yankee tenacity whose familial grip on these few precious homes was quite resolute. Frank Wilk was the caretaker of this fertile space between land and sea.

On a long, breathless, summer day, one could often find Frank in his garden, the humming bees all around, the sun high overhead, and Frank's gnarled hands, like ancient roots, massaging the dark humid soil to bring whatever he planted to life. Or on his dock, the fiddler crabs gurgling and clicking in the honeycombed bank, water lapping the shore, and Frank kneeling, with shirt sleeves rolled back, cleaning fish and casting their entrails to the blue crabs flashing up from the bottom to feed. Towards dusk, Frank could often be found in his chicken coop, where feathers and grain scented the air, and the din of clucking fowl and flapping wings would precede him as he'd shepherd his flock to their roost for the night. Frank lived by immutable laws – the rhythms of Nature – he took what he needed to survive, and he provided what she needed to flourish.

It had been a typical day for Frank, filled with tilling the earth, pruning shrubs, feeding chickens, running errands, and oiling a hinge on an old garage door. After folding the stepladder and hanging it back on a rusty nail, Frank stood by the garage and rubbed his back. "I'm old," he sighed, "No more 'getting' about it." Frank would often gripe about arthritic hands, a stiff back, and stubborn knees, but those who knew him took some salt with his grumbling, sure in their knowledge that he was one of the most content people on the face of this earth. So long as there were living things to care for, he was happy.

So it was with a father's concern that Frank looked for the hundredth time that day towards the eelgrass at the foot of a nearby embankment. For several days he'd seen a pair of geese moving in and out of the tall grass – no doubt nesting – and he kept a close watch for the goslings he was certain would come. The prior evening, however, in the twilight, Frank heard a strange sound drifting over the marsh – a muffled squawking – and he thought he had seen the silhouette of a dog. It had been late, and he was tired, so he hoped his imagination had tricked him, but the following day, having not seen the geese, his heart sank.

"Better go have a look," he muttered to himself, just as Sophie, his elder half-sister, called from the kitchen for him to come in. He and Sophie had lived together since the death of her second husband. Frank and Sophie were a team of some local renown; Christmas cards got delivered with no more address than their first names and the town.

"Frank," she hollered, not knowing where he was, "dinner is ready! Come in and wash up!"

"I'm right here," Frank grumbled. "There's no need to shout."

"Well c'mon in."

"Not now," he said. "I'll be back in a minute."

"Now where are you going?" She was used to his puttering and ready to put her foot down. "The squash will burn."

"Just take it off the stove and turn off the burner," he told her, knowing she could forget things like that. One time he came in to find smoke billowing from a pot and Sophie perched in the bay window, knitting.

"C'mon, Frank! Dinner's ready. It can wait 'til tomorrow!"

"No, it can't," he said. "I've got to see what's happened to the geese."

Uh oh, the geese, now she knew. "You didn't see them today?"

"No, I didn't," he said. "And I'm worried. I'm gonna row over and have a look."

"All right," Sophie answered. "But be careful."

"Nothing's gonna happen to me," he grumbled as took a deep breath to stoke up his energy, then he walked towards the dock.

For years the old dock had served as the launching point for Frank and Sophie's fishing adventures. Each winter Frank hauled the single float up onto the bank, and each spring he pushed it back in. Sophie's fishing boat, an old fiberglass runabout with an Evinrude motor, was tied to the outside of the float. Frank's wooden skiff, even older, was tied to one side. The skiff's insides, once varnished, were now painted over, and the bronze oarlocks were tarnished a dull brown. Frank climbed aboard, careful to center his balance in the tippy little skiff, then he sat down on the seat, set the oars in their oar-locks, untied the painter (the bowline) and pushed off.

A slight ebbing tide gently pulled the skiff's bow, and Frank dipped the oars now and then to guide his way, but mostly he drifted over the snail- and rock-speckled bottom with long strands of seaweed streaming gently with the tide. Opposite the shore where he was pretty sure the nest lay; Frank took a few pulls on the oars to get out of the current and nose-in. The eel-grass stood golden in the sun's ebbing rays, and all was silent but the water lapping against the skiff's hull and a short muffled "shwishh" as its bow nudged the embankment.

Frank gently shipped the oars, stood up, and stepped ashore with the painter. He wrapped it around a barnacled rock and stepped carefully up the bank. As expected, just a few feet beyond the reach of high tide and behind a curtain of grass, Frank found a large nest of dried grass. There were no geese to defend it, but in the nest there were eggs – three of them. Each was twice the size of a hen's egg, light gray in color, and stippled with darker gray flecks. And one egg was cracked, its life ended by whatever fracas Frank was now certain had driven off or killed the parents. But the other two were intact. He stooped to touch them, to feel for their warmth. They were cool. Not good, but they might still survive, so he knelt down and picked them up, using his shirt like a hammock to hold them.

With an athletic youth borne of need, Frank unwrapped the painter, climbed gingerly back aboard the skiff and rowed to his dock, all while cradling the eggs in his lap. Though weary just moments before, now his mind raced. How would he hatch the eggs? He would normally use the incubator he had for his chicks, but the thermostat was broken. He pondered how he might try to fix it, but then another thought struck him. He had a duck he'd adopted last year, and she had a clutch in the chicken coop. He knew just what to do.

Most of the chickens were still out in the pen – scratching the earth for a last morsel of food in the dying light – so Frank entered the coop without fuss. Even had his flock been in for the night, they seemed to think of him as just one of them and would fret very little, but this evening there were just a few hens clucking softly, as if to advise the duck on the best way to roost: 'Sit with your wings ruffled out, dear, that's how to keep the dears warm. And cluck now and then to reassure them.' Seeing Frank approach, the duck quacked and flapped her wings a few times, sending up a small cloud of feathers and dander.

"Settle down," Frank soothed. "You chickens go on out for a minute," and he shooed them out the little rubber-flap door. The duck sat there, head bobbing. "Okay," he spoke gently and showed her the eggs. "You're gonna sit on these too. You won't mind," and slowly he reached for the duck. She pecked at his hand, but Frank spoke in a mild singsong, "It's all right. It's all right. I'm not gonna hurt you. You know that." And so with soft, patient coaxing, he lifted her from the nest and placed the new eggs next to her own. When he released her, she shimmied her tail and puffed out her breast as if to say, 'My goodness,' then she re-settled herself without further complaint.

And so it was that the two rescued eggs found a warm place to spend their days, and Frank resumed the business of husbanding his little community on the edge of a salt marsh. This lasted for about two weeks, then all the eggs hatched in the space of twelve hours – four baby ducks and two goslings. The duck was as proud as could be of her brood, but for some reason the goslings decided that Frank was their mother. Perhaps it was because he was there when they hatched, or maybe they instinctively knew he had saved them. Whatever the reason, for the next several months the goslings and Frank were inseparable. No matter what chore he was doing, they would be at his feet, as faithful as any pair of dogs, and if Frank had an errand to run in town, they'd wander around the yard honking until he returned.

There's one time in particular that Frank loved to recount. The day was rainy, but he had planned to paint the inside of his skiff, so he flipped it over on a pair of sawhorses and crawled under to work. The geese crowded right under there with him. As he slathered on paint, they inspected each brush stroke, and when he'd finished, they were splattered with paint, but just being with him made them happy, and him too, as his twinkling eyes would betray when he complained, "They just wouldn't let me be!"

The goslings lived with Frank and his menagerie for more than a year, shedding their baby down and growing to goose adolescence, even taking their first flights, but always returning to the yard. Eventually, they flew out to the salt pond to land and mingle with other geese. They'd be gone for hours at a time, but always they'd return before nightfall.

Those were the days when I still spent long weekends on the Cape – visiting my grandmother – and I'd often stop by to see Frank, inspect the latest vegetables he'd harvested from his garden, and ask how the geese were doing. On one evening in particular, when the sky was clear and the stars were just beginning to wink through the sunset's glow, we talked for a while – about the weather, about life – and not seeing or hearing the geese, I asked where they were. "Oh, they're around," he replied. "Somewhere on the marsh. I'll get them."

Standing with his rake like a staff, his thin hair matted with sweat to his wrinkled forehead, his nails caked with dirt, one shirt-tail untucked, and the cuffs of his trousers crumpled down at the heels of his battered sneakers, Frank called out across the salt-marsh. "Here goosey, goosey, goosey," his voice rasped. "Here goosey, goosey!" And in the waning light of that evening, I heard the honking of geese, and in less than a minute the two of them swooped overhead and banked into a turn, circling lower until they landed a dozen feet away and ran up to Frank. He just smiled at me as if to say, 'you see, here they are.'

By the end of that summer the geese left to journey south with their wild cousins. "As it should be," Frank noted without the least sadness. And for many a summer thereafter they returned to nest on the salt march, raising their own broods and bringing them to visit. To hear Frank tell it, however, they were just a damned nuisance. "They make a mess of my lawn!" But his eyes would be smiling as he'd tell me, "Come have a look."

* * *

I can't recall exactly when I met Frank. It's like his presence in my life grew from an unnoticed seed to a wizened old apple tree that enriched my life in simple, soulful ways. Perhaps we met at some summer clambake where visiting grandkids were introduced to timeworn Cape-Codders. Certainly, I was a young boy, perhaps seven or eight, and being more interested in other kids, sandcastles, swimming, and tennis lessons, I paid little attention. But vague memories of Frank seem to begin at this time, and they grew from acquaintance to curiosity, from curiosity to fondness, and from fondness to devoted friendship. If ever I had a lost great uncle, in Frank he was found. He passed away in January 2007, 94 years young, and time marches on once again.

The Game of Kings

David Boiani

New York City 2048

Gusts of wind blew the accumulating debris into mini tornados, cluttering what remained of Fifth Avenue as Naren headed home, carefully avoiding the few parked pods occupying the edge of the sidewalk. *What happened to this city?* he thought as he rambled through the barren landscape of what previously was the heartbeat of America, if not the entire world. Heading north, he noticed the pollution overtaking the Jacqueline Kennedy Onassis Reservoir to his west as he passed. He entered what used to be Harlem and turned left onto West 118th Street, toward his small apartment on the third floor. He paused as he picked up a stray newspaper amidst the debris. *The True American* was owned and published by the last remaining self-made millionaire in the country.

Communism - we have become what our ancestors feared…

Over the last thirty years, this once proud country has evolved from a thriving capitalistic economic system to a socialistic system, now progressing into a communistic scheme seemingly overnight. My fellow Americans, we are losing on every front. Russia has beaten us at our own game: capitalism. Since the Russian discovery of the cure for cancer in stem cells, this nation has grown economically, militarily, and spiritually. Russian morale is at an all-time high while American morale continues to plummet.

Naren dropped the paper as he entered his building and bounded up the stairs to his paltry apartment, his mind spinning, knowing the importance of this day. He searched the cupboard for some crackers or cookies, but he had depleted his meager stash long ago. He fired up his laptop, the one last remaining possession of his which still held value, and typed 'The Game of Kings' into the search bar. A simplistic website loaded, decorated with a black and white chess board and all of the black and white pieces anchored at their starting points. Under the picture were a couple of prompts, one labeled "play now" and one labeled "bet." He clicked on "bet" and checked the available funds in his account. Five hundred and seven euros remained. He typed 500 into the betting window, hesitating momentarily as he knew this was his last chance. He closed his eyes as the reality of what he was about to do hit home. It was an all-or-nothing proposition: lose and he would be broke, squandering all the savings he was able to conserve over the past five years. He needed to double his funds in order to leave the country he once loved, and what better way to let it all ride but on chess, his one skill. Migrating to Russia was out of the question; however, he could live a fine life as a laborer in Canada, where his brother had escaped years ago.

He pressed "search" and the site spun, exploring the cyber-world for a match. *Success* flashed on the screen and the name Vladimir Petrov appeared. *A Russian,* he thought. The Russians were skilled at chess; however, not ever being one to back down from a challenge, Naren welcomed the confrontation. He pressed "ready" and the game was on. He donned his virtual reality headset as an animated chessboard loaded on the screen. The players controlled their pieces telepathically, without any physical activity or connection. The game had chosen Vladimir to take his turn first; however, he declined, letting Naren control white and make the initial move. Naren maneuvered his pawn forward two spots to e4 and the duel had begun. Following a few sparring moves by pawns, Naren was the first to draw blood, taking one of the Russian's pawns on d5. He heard a snap, followed by a muffled scream through his headset. Vladimir's right pinky had been snapped at the knuckle. As is true of classic chess, this new version of the game required sacrifice, not only in the pieces captured by your opponent but in the amount of pain you were willing to endure. Captured pawns were worth fingers and toes selected randomly by the artificial intelligence, knights meant tibia and fibula, bishops for the humerus, rooks took the femur, the queen your spine, and the almighty king meant the neck, and the end of the game. It was a game of pain tolerance as well as strategy. Keeping your mind clear and focused as you felt your bones shatter had become a honed skill that only the best players could master. It was all virtual reality, of course, the device on the player's head sending brain waves of pain simulating the trauma.

Naren felt his lower leg snap as the Russian took one of his knights, which caused him to grit his teeth and muffle a scream. He countered by capturing a rook, instantly followed by the large crack of a thighbone. Naren winced as two more fingers were cracked. Vladimir wailed as Naren took control, capturing a bishop, followed by a pawn on his next turn. Vladimir fought back, reducing Naren's army with every move. For over thirty minutes the two sparred, enduring a combination of sixteen broken bones between them. Naren suffered a full leg break, one arm, and six fingers and toes. The Russian lost use of both arms, both upper legs, and three fingers.

Finally, Vladimir made a crucial mistake, putting his queen in jeopardy. Naren took her and heard the loud crack of his opponent's spine followed by a shriek loud enough to pierce an eardrum. The Russian lost his ability to concentrate at that point. Naren cornered the king on h8. Checkmate, Naren was victorious. He slowly removed his headset, which had gone silent after the snapping of Vladimir's neck. *Funds transferred* flashed on the screen and Naren quickly removed his headset, basking as his broken bones ceased throbbing. He turned off the system and placed it in a bag. It was time to move.

After pawning the contents of the bag at a shop for 100 euros, Naren headed to a euro kiosk. He withdrew all his money and headed for the last remaining hyperloop in New York. On the way, he passed a homeless man and his dog. They both were starving, evidenced by their bones protruding through their skin. The canine population had been reduced dramatically over the past thirty years, as the cost of having a pet was more burden than most could endure. As the number of dogs dwindled, people started using the remaining strays for food, annihilating what was left. The dog lifted his head and let out a low whimper as Naren paused to reach down and pet him. Naren knew the animal and his owner would be dead in a few days. A tear rolled down his cheek as the memories of a different life took over his mind. A life of prosperity, family, kindness, and love. However, that was a long time ago, and this morbid reality was all that remained.

He paid the toll for the trip to Buffalo, headed for a point his brother designated and quickly boarded the hyperloop. The next fifteen minutes were the most exciting of his life. He could barely keep a straight thought in his head as he watched the northeastern United States landscape rush by. He exited the loop by foot a mere ten minutes from the border. Exhilaration grew with every step he took, his mind a jumble of thoughts, his stomach turning with nervousness and his heart filled with emotion. His thoughts turned to his family years ago, now broken and destroyed. The face of his beautiful wife filled his mind. She had passed from disease before the couple could bear children. Suddenly, the border came into sight and he could taste freedom, democracy, and prosperity. He hoped he could make it over the border, he hoped to find his brother and shake his hand, he hoped...

The Big Ride

Joanne Perella

The directions to the starting point of the bike ride had the wrong exit number, so I got lost on the way to Worcester. As a result, I arrived 35 minutes late and had barely enough time to slather sunscreen on my face, arms, and legs, check in for my ride number, and run to the porta-john where there was already a waiting line.

Opening ceremonies consisted of a cheerful guy thanking us for riding for the Cancer Society and giving us directions, most of which I missed because the sound speakers were squeaky and I was out of range. As I fastened my helmet around my chin, I looked at the other riders. I gulped when I saw most of them, fit, with biker bodies and riding bikes that cost in the thousands. My partner-in-crime Kelly and I exchanged nervous glances. We had Camelbaks with 75 ounces of water each, which weighed a ton, along with large bike packs strapped onto the back of our bikes. Everyone else had two water bottles fastened to their bikes, and a small compartment that fit behind the seat. They had wisely restricted the weight they carried. We were clearly out of our league and we slithered to the back of the line.

We were off! Bright balloons in an arch waved gently in the hot breeze as we made our way up the road to Main Street. At this point in the ride, policemen stood at intersections to block traffic to let us through. We were an impressive large pack of colorful bikers and people cheered as we rode by.

By the third or fourth mile, however, most of the riders had left us in their dust and we were riding solo. By the time we reached the next policeman, he grudgingly let us pass, annoyed that we were so far behind. Soon, we could no longer see the pack of riders at all. Kelly moaned that we were lost. I half-jokingly suggested we skip the rest of the ride and look for a place to have a big breakfast. My stomach was already growling and pancakes were on my mind. Kelly was not amused.

As it turned out, we were not lost, just really slow. Now we had to cross the busy streets by ourselves because the policemen had disappeared, probably with pancakes also on their mind. So we followed the yellow signs posted for the bike route and vowed to catch up. That is, until we spotted "Dead Horses Hill."

Legend has it that in the olden days, horses went up this hill carrying heavy logs in the hot sun. Hence, the name is a tribute to the many horses who lost their lives to this hill, which could just as easily have been named "Dead Horses Mountain." It was not a hill. It was several large hills, with no break between them. As I got to the top of the first one, gasping for breath, I was dismayed to see that the road did not level out in front of me.

In fact, the road never leveled off. Despite the assurances of the Cancer Society's cheerful volunteers that the ride only had "one large hill," the ride was almost all uphill. Not gently rolling hills, as pictured in travel books. These were steep climbs, not for the fainthearted. Nor were they for the occasional spinner and/or recreational bike rider whose longest ride was a flat easy ride on a bike path by the sea. Like me.

By the time I reached the first water station 23 miles later, I needed a cold shower, ice water, and a rest, in that order. People looked at me anxiously, expecting me to drop any minute. But another cheerful Cancer Society worker told me that it is "now all downhill from here." Like a fool, I believed her.

There were big white "SAG" (Support and Gear) trucks that drove around to make sure riders were okay. The rule was to give them a thumbs up if you were fine, or a thumbs down if you needed some help. I didn't know this, since it was part of the instructions I missed during the opening ceremonies. As a result, SAG trucks kept slowing down beside me with annoyed looks because I wasn't giving them a thumb, either up or down. Instead, I was sorely tempted to have them give me a lift to the finish line.

The route we took from Worcester to Boston College must have been designed by a geography dropout. Instead of going east, we went south, and west, and north, twisting around towns in Massachusetts that I never knew existed. At one point, at the top of a hill (naturally), I stopped to gulp down some water and a gummy gel pack (for energy). I saw a farmer working with his cows and horses and I asked him where I was. He said I was in Sutton and asked me where I was going. I was tempted to say no place but I answered Boston College. He said, "Oh, are you lost then?" I laughed and told him that was the understatement of the year.

Somehow, I managed to get to the next water station, taking rest breaks along the way. Most of the time I was completely alone, since everyone else was either far ahead of me or broken down behind me. Once, one of the SAG drivers asked me if I had seen a guy in a red shirt. He was one of the riders who was lost and unaccounted for. I wondered where he was and pictured him lost in the tangle of woods, down some country road in the middle of nowhere.

The miles slowly went by. I caught up with others at the water station and we compared stories. Kelly fell behind after a while and we rode together. But it was hard to converse while riding because the hills frequently made us breathless and exhausted. I began to take more and more rest stops, plopping down on brick walls and gulping down water. One elderly couple came out of their sprawling mansion on the edge of a pond somewhere, carrying lemonade for me. They asked me if I wanted to use their phone, as if I were a homeless person. I was touched by their concern and generosity.

At the last water station, they were packing up for the day. Most of the riders had already reached the finish line and gone home. The SAG trucks were removing the yellow signposts from the trees, assuming no one needed directions any longer. It was now eight miles to the finish line. We gulped down ice water, ate a few bites of a blueberry bagel and climbed on our bikes for the last time.

When we reached Wellesley, sweaty, hot, and with our legs cramping painfully, we finally felt a surge of hope. We were facing the big hill of Commonwealth Avenue, which was no comparison to the hills we already had climbed. I pedaled furiously, knowing the end was near. At the next turn, the cancer volunteers waved us into Boston College and I spotted the familiar arch of balloons ahead. My eyes filled with tears of joy and relief; I made it. And right behind me was the guy in the red shirt, looking exhausted, but happy.

A Hymn for a Memory

Steven R. Porter

I don't recall the time of day
Nor the temper of the sky

I don't recall the dress she wore
Nor the sights that passed us by

I don't recall the route we walked
Nor where we chose to shop

I don't recall how much we laughed
Nor why I chose to stop

I don't recall the argument
In which I lost my mind

I don't recall our final words
As her hand let go of mine

I don't recall how much I wept
To soothe my forlorn soul

I don't recall how long it took
To claim my self-control

You can't remember everything
Time's march steals a lot

But I do recall -- oh, quite clearly
These things that I forgot.

The Albatross

Kevin Duarte

It was exactly 5:55pm when Julia, the hostess, saw the uniformed soldier make his way through the front door of the restaurant. She immediately recognized the formal army attire the soldier was wearing, complete with beret, shoulder chords, and an array of decorations pinned above both front pockets on his chest. The soldier stood in the open doorway while the wind and snow howled outside. Without an overcoat, but unfettered by the cold, he held the door open for a couple leaving the restaurant. He nodded as they walked past, then walked in, closed the door, and quietly waited for Julia's attention. Julia had just turned twenty, and the soldier looked like he wasn't more than a decade older.

"Reservation?" Julia inquired in a warm friendly voice.

"Schaffer," replied the soldier congenially. He offered Julia the slightest of smiles. She pulled up the reservation on the screen at her podium, then gave an inquisitive look.

"The reservation is only for one person?" she asked.

"Yes, ma'am," replied the soldier.

"No one to celebrate with?"

"It's not a celebration," replied the soldier. His expression became more subdued, and he dropped his eyes toward the floor. "More of a memorial."

Julia cringed at her own inquiry. "I'm sorry."

"No need to apologize, ma'am," the soldier replied. "I invited some others, but they informed me that they were not able to attend."

Only slightly consoled, Julia grabbed a menu from her station and led the soldier through the dining area. He followed her to a small, two-person table next to a far wall by a window. She placed the menu on the elegant white tablecloth next to the exquisitely polished silverware and spotless glasses.

"Your waiter will be with you in a moment," she said. Then she added, "Let me know if there is anything I can get you." He nodded with a cordial smile, then pulled out his chair as Julia slowly started back to her station.

The soldier noticed another of the waitstaff as he approached the table. A man a few years older than himself, he carried a pitcher of water and a menu that was slimmer than the one placed on the table by the hostess.

"I'm Greg, your waiter," he greeted as he filled one of the glasses on the table. He handed the soldier a tall, thin menu. "This is a list of our drinks if you are interested…"

"None for me, thank you, sir," replied Schaffer as he waved off the menu. Greg smoothly slid it under his left arm and continued.

"Would you like to hear the specials that we have this evening?" inquired the waiter.

"I've already decided," replied the soldier. "I'll have the albatross. I read on your website yesterday that you were offering it on your menu this week. Is that correct?"

"As a matter of fact, we are," replied Greg, somewhat surprised. Rarely offered, the menu item was the restaurant's foray into untraditional poultry items. Other bistros in the area were trying their hand at unconventional menu items, so to maintain their competitive edge, the restaurant had embarked on the same strategy. But Greg could count on one hand the number of times this particular species was ordered.

"Wonderful," replied the soldier.

"Can I get you anything else with that?" inquired the waiter. "An appetizer maybe?"

"No, sir," replied Schaffer.

"Alright then, I'll place your order right away," replied the waiter. After a cordial smile and a quick nod Greg was off, leaving the soldier to himself.

Hands pressed together in front of his face, Schaffer rested his jaw on his thumbs as his eyes scanned the restaurant. The dining area was relatively quiet for a Thursday evening. The tables were predominantly occupied by couples, except for one long table at the far end of the restaurant that was surrounded by a dozen older gentlemen. The loudest of all the tables, the men were engaged in banter and laughter, and seemed to Schaffer as if it was a reunion. He looked closely and noticed that some of the men wore baseball caps. Although quite informal for the establishment, the insignias on the hats were from the Air Force, and – at least to Schaffer – did not appear to be inappropriate.

Schaffer sat quietly at his table, staring blankly, lost in recollection, except for the intermittent moments when his attention seemed drawn to the camaraderie of the table across the room. A coy smile stretched across his face as he heard the stories of the veterans unfolding with youthful energy and abandon. Skewed and exaggerated recollection of shared events led to laughter and a revitalized camaraderie as they reflected on their victories and spoils, not the least of which was their ability to make it home from the foreign lands which they reluctantly inhabited for years. They had been caught up and transplanted from their homes by the big campaign of worldly conflict, and had returned relatively unscathed.

Schaffer remembered the servicemen he had worked with during his Special Ops days. The mission he was on exactly one year ago was the one that was vivid in his mind. He remembered it clearly, and was honoring it with the meal he had ordered. Looking at empty chair at his table, Schaffer wished that some of his squad-mates could have accompanied him at this dinner. The reasons for them not appearing, in Schaffer's mind, were war-ranted.

Logistics. Commitments. And of course, death.

Casualties of combat.

Half of Schaffer's squad had died a year ago. Two of the men who were lost were soldiers he had trained with at Fort Bragg. They had toured together on several missions in the deserts of Iran and Afghanistan. Schaffer himself was a demolitions expert. His friends - one a weapons sergeant, the other an intelligence officer specializing in intelligence gathering and target analysis – were the best in their respected areas, as was Schaffer. Trained and honed to razor sharpness by the military, they were hand-picked for the mission by the Detachment Commander himself, which each of them deemed an honor.

One of the Air Force veterans got up from his table and started to the lavatory, making his way past the table where Schaffer sat. The veteran nodded, then walked into the men's room. Upon his return, he noticed the soldier still sitting by himself.

"Apologies for intruding," said the veteran. "What's a fine young man like you doing sitting by yourself?"

Schaffer turned toward the man. "Just having a meal, sir."

"You all by yourself?" asked the veteran.

"Yes sir," replied Schaffer.

"The name's Barnes," replied the veteran, then with a laugh added, "and you can save that 'sir' crap for your COs back at your base." He tapped the front of his hat. "Air Force. Fifteen years of service."

Schaffer got up from his chair and extended his hand while thanking the veteran for his service. Barnes shook the soldier's hand, his attention drawn to the beret on the table.

"They don't hand those caps out to just anyone," Barnes said with a respectful nod. "You should be proud of that. I've known some very tough Green Berets in my time."

"As have I," replied Schaffer humbly. Barnes laughed and tapped Schaffer on the shoulder. He turned to his table, took a step, then turned back toward the soldier.

"Come join us," urged the veteran. "Share some war stories with a bunch of crusty old veterans."

"I appreciate the offer," replied Schaffer. "But I've already ordered."

"Suit yourself," replied the veteran. "If you change your mind, come on by the table."

Schaffer nodded to the veteran, who tilted his baseball cap to him, then turned and headed back to his table. Greg passed the veteran as he headed to Schaffer's table with his meal. He carefully placed the plate of food in front of the soldier, then was gone.

Schaffer gazed at the meal, as if it contained something more to him than just a source of nourishment. He took a deep breath, carefully unwrapped his silverware, then placed his napkin in his lap. The succulent white meat was eloquently garnished with the slightest bit of parsley and olives. Tilting his head as he bent over the meal, Schaffer seemed very tentative about cutting open the meat. He looked up from the plate as if trying to find Greg, but the waiter was in the back room retrieving another order. Schaffer picked up his glass of water, took a long drink, then carefully placed the glass back on the table.

Julia watched as ever so delicately the soldier sliced down the middle of the bird that had been prepared for him. He separated the meat at the incision, and then abruptly placed his utensils on the table beside the plate.

Greg, as was his routine, came by only a few minutes after the plate was served to check on the guest. Schaffer's expression was that of slight confusion and mild disappointment.

"Is everything okay?" asked Greg as he reached the table.

"This doesn't look right," replied the soldier. "Are you sure this is what I ordered?"

"You ordered the albatross, correct?" replied Greg.

"Yes, sir," replied Schaffer.

"I can check with the chef, but I'm extremely confident that this is what he made for you."

"If you could check with him, sir, that would be great," replied Schaffer.

Greg dashed into the kitchen, and before the dark, heavy door even came to a rest, the waiter came back through and headed to the table.

"That is the albatross," replied Greg. "Should I get you something else?"

"No. No," replied Schaffer. "I hate to be a bother, especially since this is the meal that brought me to the restaurant."

"Let me know if I can get you anything," Greg said. And with that he was off.

Schaffer sliced into the meat again but refused to spear it with a fork and bring any of the meat up to his mouth. Barnes watched from a distance, then rose from his table and walked over. He could tell that there was something not right about the food he had ordered.

"Everything okay there, son?" asked Barnes.

"This doesn't look like the albatross I had a year ago," answered Schaffer.

"What's different about it?"

"The one I had was redder than this," replied the soldier as he turned the meat with his knife. Barnes turned to Greg and signaled him to come to the table. The waiter appeared, and he was informed of the problem.

"There are many bird species that look more like meat," replied Greg. "Maybe what you had was really a pigeon breast. Now that looks like a cut of beef rather than a piece of chicken. We actually have some here if you would like to try some."

Schaffer turned and without a word, simply nodded his head. Sweat started to form at his brow. The veteran noticed the soldier's disposition and sat at the table. Schaffer looked like he needed some kind of distraction, which Barnes provided.

"Where are you stationed?" the veteran asked.

"Fort Carson," replied Schaffer as he gently pushed the plate of food away.

"In Colorado. Nice," replied Barnes. "Is that where they served you the albatross?"

"The food had nothing to do with where I was stationed," replied Schaffer. "I was on a mission."

"What kind of mission?" asked the veteran.

"The kind that people aren't supposed to know about," replied Schaffer, raising his head so he could lock eyes with his inquisitor. The soldier's gaze was stern but reserved.

Barnes peered back with similar intensity. "We've been on many of those type of missions ourselves."

The soldier took a deep breath and turned his head in contemplation.

"It was a year ago," Schaffer conceded as he started his narrative. "We were on a mission of intelligence gathering. I'm not at liberty to divulge the location."

The veteran nodded understandably, then slid the chair closer.

"We were in a transport plane in the middle of nowhere. We weren't expecting any opposition, and until the very last minute of the flight, we didn't get any. We were flying over a desolate mountain range in the middle of winter," Schaffer continued, his body releasing a quiver as he recalled the scenario with vivid accuracy. "We were fifty miles from the nearest base when all of a sudden we were hit by a SAM."

"Those surface-to-air missiles are nasty stuff?" added Barnes. Having been a fighter pilot himself, he knew this all too well.

"Yes they are," replied the soldier. "Took out the tail of the plane and half of one of the ailerons. Our pilot managed to put the plane down in one piece, but we were forced to crash land in the mountains."

A shiver ran up Schaffer's back that made him twitch.

"Two of our men died on impact," added Schaffer solemnly. "The communication systems were damaged, and the back of the plane snapped off. We were left exposed to the elements with half a plane as a shelter."

"Sounds like quite a predicament, son," replied Barnes.

"It was," continued Schaffer. Greg interrupted the conversation as he brought out the breast of pigeon. The veteran worried that this interruption would disrupt the flow of conversation.

Schaffer quietly thanked the waiter for the second service and peered at the seared pigeon. As described, it consisted of two small pieces of flesh, so deep red in color that it looked like it could have been a piece of steak. Its flesh was lean and, cooked medium rare, sliced open easily. Schaffer pulled the knife across the meat and peered at the incision.

"This doesn't look right, either," added the soldier. He slid the plate away and replaced it with the albatross.

"Well, even though you were in a rough predicament, it looks like you got out of there unscathed," commented Barnes. "I've been in a few tough spots myself," he added. He took the plate with the pigeon breast and handed it to Greg. "Get me another drink there, partner. And get my friend here whatever he wants."

"I'm all set, sir," replied the soldier. "But thank you."

"So how long were you up in the mountains?" asked the veteran.

"Two weeks. The wind and snow were coming into the back of the plane. It was freezing. Made today's weather seem like a spring day. We moved the bodies of our dead to a place away from the plane. Didn't even get a chance to bury them because the snow was too deep and the ground was frozen, or consisted mostly of rock, or both. We burned some of the flammables on the plane to keep warm at night when the temperature really dropped. During the day we had to rely on getting as much sunlight as possible to stay warm. After five days we ran out of the food rations we had in the plane. Our commanding officer said he was going to head out with one other squad member and try to find some food. He said he saw something flying around the area and wanted to go take a look."

"Arctic birds?" asked the veteran.

"Albatross, specifically," replied the soldier. "We heard a few gunshots off in the distance after the officers left. They came back a while later with slices of meat. We cooked it on a makeshift hotplate we constructed from pieces of the plane and some of the gear we had on board. For three days we lived on that food." Schaffer looked down at the meal before him. "That bird saved my life."

"You saved your own life," replied Barnes.

"If it wasn't for finding that food, we wouldn't have had enough strength to try and make it down to the bottom of the mountain," added the soldier. "We walked for two days with the rations and water that we gathered up. We found a small village – an outpost really - and got some communication out to one of our bases. The next day a helicopter came and brought us back to base."

"And here you are," added Barnes.

"Here I am," returned the solder. "Trying to figure out why this meal I have before me is not reminding me of the bird that miraculously provided sustenance for myself and my surviving teammates."

"Maybe it's just the way it was prepared?" said Barnes. "It's not like you had a modern kitchen to prepare the bird."

"I don't think that's it," replied the soldier. "The meat we had was darker than this but not as red as the pigeon. Looked more like pork."

"At least you found something," replied Barnes.

Schaffer contemplated for a moment, then turned to Barnes and asked, "Fifteen years in the Air Force?"

"Yes sir."

"That's a long time," added Schaffer. "Must have seen a lot of stuff go down, didn't you?"

"Of course," replied Barnes.

"Have you ever had an instance when you didn't believe what a commanding officer was telling you?" asked the soldier.

"We weren't trained that way," replied Barnes.

"Neither were we. Follow orders… to the letter."

"It's how the military system works," added Barnes.

"But you think they would have told us the truth, given the circumstances," added Schaffer, looking the veteran straight in the eyes.

"They tell us whatever we need to know to do our jobs," replied Barnes.

"They tell us only what we need to do our jobs," corrected Schaffer.

"It's not up to us to know everything to do our jobs," replied Barnes. "That's for the upper brass. They need to know to facilitate the overall objective. To get the job done."

"Or to survive," added Schaffer.

"Survival is the name of the game, isn't it?" asked Barnes.

"Yes, it is," replied Schaffer. "But we should know the cost of that survival."

"The cost?"

"Yes, the cost," replied Schaffer. He nodded toward the table of veterans across the room. "During your service, what would you be willing to sacrifice to save their lives?"

"I'd give anything to save them," replied Barnes without hesitation.

"Would you sacrifice yourself?" asked Schaffer.

"Of course," replied Barnes.

"I did survive my mission last year," replied Schaffer. "But up until now I didn't know the cost. My commanding officers on that mission knew, but they never told me, and I had a right to know."

Then, somberly, Schaffer carefully removed the medals that adorned his chest and slid them on the table next to his beret.

"What are you doing?" inquired Barnes. "You earned those metals, son."

"My squad-mates sacrificed themselves for those medals, in a way I have just come to realize."

"What do you mean?"

Schaffer looked at the meal before him, then balled a fist to his mouth as his body convulsed. His eyes watered in response and he suppressed the vomit that tried to escape his empty stomach.

"Are you okay?" asked Barnes, reaching over to the soldier.

"My officers didn't want to come here today because they didn't want to be here when I realized what they did," the soldier explained.

"What are you talking about?"

"I've never had albatross before," said Schaffer. "My commanding officers knew I'd realize that once I came to this restaurant."

"Then what was it they brought you when they went out for the hunt?" asked the veteran.

"There was no albatross up in those mountains," added Schaffer.

A look of shock and horror adorned Barnes' face as he too realized what Schaffer had already deduced. Schaffer could tell by the veteran's expression that he had also been enlightened.

"Oh my God," gasped Barnes.

"That's right," replied Schaffer. "The officers never found an albatross. All that was up there in the mountains, left to rot alone in the mountains, were the bodies of my squad-mates."

Schaffer slid the plate toward the center of the table. He rose, pulled out a hundred dollar bill from his wallet and placed it next to his beret. Leaving Barnes alone at the table, the soldier turned and headed for the door, the cold of the snow and wind hitting his face as he exited the building into the darkest of nights.

Surprised

Marjorie Turner Hollman

I shouldn't have been surprised. There was a reason he had been given the name he had, but my only thought was that I finally made it on to the back of a horse, in a riding ring near my home, ready for my first lesson.

The instructor adjusted the stirrups to fit my short little nine-year-old legs, as I fidgeted in the saddle. Two instructors stood in the middle of the ring to keep a close eye out as the class walked our horses around the ring. Because of the damp, one woman had donned a raincoat. She turned to see us better, the wind blowing open the flaps of her coat. As the fabric snapped in the wind, Surprise shied, nearly dislodging me from the saddle. I grabbed the horn of the western-style saddle, not realizing I had dropped both reins.

Surprise, on the other hand, was quite aware there was no longer anyone in the driver's seat, as it were. Given free rein, he took off like a shot. The outer rail of the riding ring looked so temptingly close. I lunged, desperate to get off this freight train of a horse.

Missed! Now this was a different perspective, as I clung to the side of Surprise, who continued his race around the ring in full gallop. In retrospect, sitting on top of the horse seemed like a better place to be, but there was no going back. As my mount galloped about the ring, the adults chased us, without success.

Surprise and I offered a circus show for my enraptured fellow students. As I sped by, wide open mouths gaped at our spectacle. In one last desperate move to dislodge me (I may have been screaming, perhaps making the situation a wee bit worse), Surprise suddenly veered left. This sneaky maneuver sent me soaring face first into a large mud puddle inside the ring. Once relieved of his noisy burden, Surprise pulled up to a stop, his ribs heaving in and out, as the instructors grabbed up his reins and led him out of the ring. Surprise would carry no more students at that riding establishment.

Strong arms lifted me upright. The instructor wiped down my face and shirt with a rough towel, the one used to dry the horses after lessons. "If you don't get back up now, you never will," the instructor warned. This advice offered little comfort in the moment. But having often reflected on this experience, I realize she did the right thing. Despite my protests, up I went onto the back of the most placid horse at the establishment, which plodded around the ring with me on its back, the instructor holding the horse's head the entire outing.

Wary but undeterred by this first adventure, I continued taking lessons that year, and later took lessons at several other stables in the area. In all that time no other horse offered a ride that came even close to my first misadventure on Surprise. I developed a taste for the rocking and rolling gait that is cantering. I preferred it to the bumpity-bump of trotting, with its attendant jarring of every bone in my body. Although the footwork for the horse is akin to galloping, cantering is mostly galloping, in first gear. For the rider, it is the difference between nestling in a big, wide rocking chair, as opposed to clinging atop a speeding freight train.

As an adult, I still loved the rocking sensation of moving atop a horse, but the possibility of disaster, especially with an unfamiliar steed, always lurked in my imagination. Perhaps if I'd had the chance to spend time mucking out, feeding, saddling, and generally handling a horse, my anxiety might have been assuaged.

Health issues later made riding, and even walking, more difficult for me. While I enjoyed the sensation of riding a horse, I didn't miss the worry of losing control of such a large animal. I put the option of horseback riding into the box where I'd placed so many other life experiences—something to let go of and try hard not to look back on.

One weekend, with my extended family, I visited some friends in Maine at their lakeside cottage. While there, I spotted some small, sit-on-top recreational kayaks. My children, siblings, and parents climbed into the kayaks at this quiet lake, eased out into the water, and soon headed off to explore parts of the lake I could only long to see, stranded on the shore. Unlike river kayaks, these small boats are quite stable and easy to steer, intended for leisurely paddles in calm waters, not for dashing through white water rapids. Despite my mobility issues, I needed to try one of these little boats. They looked just my speed.

With help, I soon found myself atop a purple kayak, and pushed out into the water. The gentle rocking sensation brought me back in a flash, to times when I sat atop a calm, gentle horse, gliding, as horses do, over the ground, in a gentle canter. Only this time, it was a kayak, floating close to the water's surface, rocking gently with each small wave that slid underneath us. How much easier it would be to look after this "steed," with no risk of being stepped on, bit, or even run away with! And no need to feed or care for the craft, once tucked away on shore.

A motorboat drove by, sending a rolling wake in my direction. The kayak and I easily rode the swells, just as I had when my horse was urged to a canter. I hated to return to shore. Despite my substantial mobility challenges, I had found a way to move once more with grace. A surprise, for sure.

Once back home near Silver Lake, south of Boston, I kept thinking about that little kayak, and the pleasure I'd had paddling it. Turns out, my siblings had been thinking the same thing. They recognized my joy, and soon my sister arrived with a bright red kayak for me. We took it out on Silver Lake to christen it. My boat, Lil Red, has since traveled many miles with me.

On one of the first dates my future husband and I shared, we paddled our kayaks together on the Sudbury River, near where he lived. There we discovered our mutual joy in the outdoors, as well as our shared passion of being on the water in our little watercraft. Floating along the river, we passed others quietly paddling by in their kayaks and canoes. Conversation flowed easily between us as we followed the course of the river, playfully bumping each other's boats as we wandered from shore to shore, exploring the waterway. Great blue herons played hide and seek among the grasses, soaring on giant wingspans just ahead of us, then settling down, complaining loudly as we approached. Shy turtles performed quick nosedives into the water as we paddled close to their sunny rocks and logs.

These days we still seek out quiet waterways, and are always on the lookout for rivers and lakes to explore in our kayaks. A recently added tandem kayak increased our small flotilla. A sleek vessel that steers easily, the tandem allows us to travel together, our paddles knifing through the water in rhythm.

The day I first settled into the seat of that little kayak in Maine, I was surprised and delighted, quite differently than on my first encounter with a horse in the riding ring. With each stroke of my paddle, I was almost overwhelmed with the sensation that I was back on horseback, yet grateful for the differences. Turns out I had been searching for a little boat to love all along.

When life feels hard, my kayak provides a refuge, a comfort, until I'm ready to face the day. Alone or with companions, my heart sings, gliding atop the gentle waves that roll underneath me. How lucky (and surprising) for me, in the past number of years, that I have found other ways to move, much more suited to my temperament and abilities.

I am convinced that everyone needs a "little boat" in their life. Mine is waiting at the lake. And as far as I can tell, my kayak has never even thought of running away with me.

Army of One

Rick Roberts

My love story with the US Army began with a letter in 1968. The correspondence explained that President Lyndon Johnson had repealed most graduate school deferments. Specifically, if I was making a crucial contribution to the defense and well-being of America — let's say engineering better airflow over the blades of a Sikorsky H-34 helicopter, then I could stay in school. But I was just working on a master's degree in journalism at The University of Iowa. *Pack your bags, private.* The letter generously allowed that I could complete the semester before reporting. It was a friendly letter, really. The kind one might get from an uncle who needed a favor.

Three months later, right before the semester ended, a second letter arrived. The tone was less conciliatory and more to the point. At the top it said "Order To Report For Induction" in hard-to-miss letters.

As luck would have it, my parents had moved in the interim, from suburban Philadelphia to Scottsdale, Arizona. And the law back then provided the right to be drafted from your official home address. Swapping draft boards would buy me time. Besides, Arizona sent its draftees to Fort Ord, California — much more desirable than training in the muck of Fort Bragg, North Carolina, my likely destination if called up out of Pennsylvania. Things were almost looking up. I sent back a friendly note of my own, informing the government of my new hometown.

It took Uncle Sam two months to adjust. The third offer for a free olive drab wardrobe reached my parents' mailbox in Scottsdale in mid-March of 1969. Perhaps suspecting that I was contemplating an extended vacation in Canada, the army gave me just 48 hours to report. I was still in Iowa City, quietly hoping they had lost track of me. Meanwhile, my parents were in Los Angeles that week and when they finally reached me with the news, the 48-hour deadline had passed.

I sent off a jaunty explanation. I explained I had no way of knowing when I might be re-drafted after the address change. Naturally, I decided to remain in graduate school and was now well into my second semester. Surely the army didn't expect me to waste this effort, nor the time and money associated with it. I wanted to serve my country, I wrote, just like the men in my family had done before me. I wasn't a draft dodger, more of a draft postponer. I was coming, I just found the suggested timing a tad inconvenient. I was thinking more like this summer. How would that be?

They promptly drafted me for April.

This time, the bottom of the notice detailed my obligation under the Selective Service statutes and a list of penalties associated with failing to comply. Democracy isn't free, I was reminded. Nevertheless, I needed more time. I had just spent the year submerged in the intellectual delights that abound in Big Ten university towns, not to mention the company of a comely undergrad, a former "tulip queen," and proto-typical descendant of the northern European pioneers who reached Iowa a hundred years earlier, scooped up a handful of black dirt, and wisely stayed to work the richest topsoil on the continent. I never met an Iowan who didn't own at least 160 fertile acres. I've never seen corn so tall.

It was a peaceful and well-mannered place even in the rock 'n'roll 60s. The locals were circumspect about the temptations of fashion; they taught me what was funny about *Green Acres*; and if you had a hankering for a new refrigerator, a mug of real German beer or the sound of zither music, the Amana colonies were up the road a piece. When I arrived that fall, the talk on campus wasn't about Vietnam; rather, Hawkeye football. The idea of slogging through the jungle with a 70-pound pack on my back alert for folks who wanted to kill me would require a mind-expanding, make that mind-blowing, transition and none of the drugs I was doing at the time were up to the job.

When I didn't show up in April, they drafted me in May.

And again in June. By now the messages were as short as telegrams and the tone downright officious. On the bottom of the sixth one, someone had scribbled, "Better get your ass down here." Meanwhile, I was papering the bathroom wall with the notices, which amused neither parent. In Mother's eyes it was a decorating faux pas, to my brown-boot father something more akin to treason.

Here's what you needed to know to survive back then: they were drafting 25 to 30 thousand guys a week. The war had dragged on for years and they were simply running out of bodies. It was self-defeating for the draft board to take me out of the eligibility pool.

They didn't have the manpower to prosecute you anyway. My strategy: keep talking to them. Convince them how much I, too, loved my country. I told you, this is a love story.

By June I'd adjusted to the desert heat in Arizona and tried hard to get my mind right. I studied philosophy as an undergraduate and fell back on that instruction, especially Plato, who'd written extensively on the morality of citizenship. I accepted the position that my country had the right to draft me, and I didn't have the right to pick my war. I had ruled Canada out early on — too big a decision for a 23-year old. Likewise with shooting off my little toe, though I knew one guy who did. My best friend threw down enough controlled substances, legal and otherwise, to fail the urine and blood tests, then insisted on sitting on top of the psych profiler's desk cross-legged and chanting during the interview. They knew he wasn't nuts, but he was too much trouble. 4-F! Not foxhole-worthy. Forget the mounting public distress over our unconscionable behavior in Vietnam, the student protests I'd participated in, the hollow promises of our leaders — I was about to change teams.

My feet weren't flat, my back was straight, and I was at the height of my physical prowess from running cross country and distance track for years in school. Heck, if you were warm and upright, you were in. They loved sure-shot guys like me.

A-1 all the way. Mother tried to help at the last minute, asking me to clean out the nests of black widow spiders residing the pool shed. I don't know if she was

secretly hoping I'd get bit, but I sure was. A headline declaring "Local man dies in a fair fight with dangerous bugs" had more appeal than a missing-in-action report.

"Hanging around the pool drinking beer isn't going to make this go away," Dad opined over BBQ one otherwise pleasant afternoon.

* * *

It was already ninety-five degrees in the Valley of the Sun the morning I reported for duty. About fifty of us were shuffled through a series of administrative tasks and preliminary examinations. Mid-morning, we were herded into an expansive men's room and handed a small plastic cup with our name and new US Army identification number on it. They wanted a urine sample, and there was a process. Work it up, and proceed to the next station. If not, stand at a urinal and flush it repeatedly until the power of suggestion moved me. If that didn't work, run my hands under a warm sink faucet, re-grab my truculent organ and strangle it into submission. Still no sample? See those unfriendly sergeants standing over there? They would escort me into the back room and reliably scare the piss out of me. Participation was one hundred percent, and I soon learned there was a proven process for everything. Getting up, going to bed, peeling potatoes. The army is a results-oriented organization.

Lunch was provided via coupon at the diner next door. I was about halfway through a tuna sandwich when the kid sitting across from me suddenly and violently pinned an unlucky cockroach to the wall with his fork. It didn't die.

For those who don't know, the bugs in Arizona are huge. Movie-prop-sized. Beetles the size of small birds. Shiny black on the outside and filled with cups of brown mushy guts. They hit windshields like an apple pie. There are snakes everywhere, tarantulas, poisonous lizards, and if you water your grass, scorpions and their nearest relatives stop by. Folks don't run around in bare feet and they don't pick up things in the dark out of curiosity. The speared cockroach was still fighting for his life as I got up to leave.

After lunch we assembled in an auditorium that had a stand of flags up front where several officers milled around. We all knew what was coming. That irreversible moment when you symbolically raise your right hand, take a step forward, and pledge that you're willing to die for your country. I don't know about the others, but that wasn't what was in my heart that day. We were all headed for Nam and we knew it. We had all had our lives interrupted and our futures thrown into jeopardy to participate in what was becoming a lost cause. America, in fact, had financed the war when the French fought and lost it back in the 50s, then took over despite warnings from our own generals not to commit land forces in Southeast Asia. But the heady Harvard gang around John Kennedy convinced the young president they could manage anything, even victory. They even had a theory — the Domino Theory, which held that if we didn't stop the Chinese here, we'd be fighting them on the beaches of Australia. In fact, the Chinese and Vietnamese had been at each other's throats for a thousand years and China already had enough problems controlling their billion-plus population. They were hardly in the market for more hostile citizens. So much for Ivy League military intelligence. By the time Johnson inherited the mess, we were getting our asses kicked, and the only thing on a draftee's mind was how to avoid being the last sad sack to come home in a body bag.

With pledging done, we sat down in a collective daze. But it wasn't over. In marched a Marine officer in full dress uniform who shared a few words with the

Army guys up front. Seems the Marines couldn't attract enough volunteers to fulfill their missions in 1969. Kids who might have volunteered had been drafted

into the army, or were among thousands that had rushed to fill the reserve ranks of all four military branches hoping never to see active duty. Many were repulsed by the idea that defending freedom apparently involved slaughtering women and children and turning a country of natural wonders into a toxic wasteland.

No matter, and not legal, but the army let the marines cherry-pick new draftees. The marine officer scanned the room as everyone scrunched down in their seats. He picked the kid right next to me, who looked over in dismay as he got up. "Fuck, I'll never make it," he said. He was headed for the notorious base called Camp Pendleton to become one of the nation's few good men. I was headed for Monterey, Big Sur, and Fort Ord. Heck, the Monterey Pop Festival had taken place just a few weeks before. Woodstock was in the air! And as Joan

Didion had reassured us boomers in *Slouching Towards Bethlehem*, "California is a place in which a boom mentality and a sense of Chekhovian loss meet in uneasy suspension; in which the mind is troubled by some buried but ineradicable suspicion that things better work here, because here, beneath the immense bleached sky, is where we run out of continent."

So far, so good.

* * *

On a Sunday not long after I'd been drafted during my first semester at Iowa, we were having a family dinner at my grandparents' home in upstate Pennsylvania. My father at the time was enjoying a big career with General Electric Company in the Missile and Space Vehicle Division headquartered in Valley Forge. GE was making the guidance systems and protective nose cone coverings for our newest rockets and spaceships. The space race was on, and GE rode the patriotic wave all the way to the moon. Dad spent much of his time at the White Sands Proving Grounds in New Mexico watching "the birds fly" and there were often GE vice presidents sitting around the dining room table at home. We even got a Christmas card from the White House one year.

My grandfather, who had served in WWI, a tragedy by most any measure, turned to my father before dinner and asked, "Why don't you get him out of this?"

My father, who had been in WWII, arguably a hero's war, looked at his father and in the succinct fashion that made him a visionary engineer and a crackerjack communicator, smiled thinly and said, "You went. I went. He goes."

Mother was silent through much of dinner, and cried on the ride home. Dad and I never talked about Vietnam then, nor before he died at 92.

And where, as it turned out, I never went.

Two Twains on a Train

Rick Billings

I once saw two Twains on a train.
One was eccentric,
the other insane.
As I stood on the platform I thought "Such a shame,
waiting in line with two Twains for a train..."

I searched for a seat as the first Twain brushed by.
He studied me with a casual eye.
You can guess my concern as I heard his long sigh.
Looking for seats as two Twains walked on by.

One Twain toward the front, looking obtuse,
The other in back with a little grey goose.
Two Twains on a train aloof on the loose,
One in the engine, one the caboose.

In the dining car I sat with my dish.
Twain one and Twain two had a plate of blue fish,
with Brussels and Knockwurst and Clams Cavendish!
Two Twains on a train, both sharing a Knish.

On the roof in the rain with two Twains nearby,
"Look out! A bridge!" I exclaimed with a cry.
Twain one ducked down low, Twain two jumped up high,
Two Twains on a train, one wet and one dry.

I sat in a sulk.
I stood in a snit.

I don't like these Twains, not one little bit!
I don't like their manners! Their arrogant wit! Their pithy snide comments!
One stands while Two sits!
Two Twains on this train and I'm tied to be fit!

Twain Two looked sad and said with dismay,
"What could we have done to affect you this way?
"We're handsome and suave,
with quick repartee,
We're Twains on this train - so what do you say?"

Well, I looked at those Twains,
In a new, better light.
Perhaps I was harsh?
Too rude this dark night?
They *were* a bit wry,
And had far-out insight.
Two Twains on this train,
Perhaps they were right?

Well, I may have been hasty,
and I may have been rash,
a little distracted by Twain Two's
moose-tache.
They were a bit wry,
their manner quite brash.
Two Twains on this train,
Bound for old Calabash.

"Yo ho!" said Twain One. "He's getting it now!"
Twain Two stood up tall, did a half-twist kowtow.
"We're *so* pleased to have you among the lowest high brow!"
"We Twains on this train welcome you with a bow!"

We played pigeon toss,
Three-way solitaire,

The Twains were well versed and could quote Baudelaire.
After trying on hats,
and dyeing our hair,
those two Twains and I,
we made quite a pair.

We belted out chanteys,
played Jacks Acey-Deuce,
threw paint at blank canvas,
like Vermeer and Toulouse.
We studied all subjects,
learning to be obtuse,
then we Twains on this train
schmoozed in the caboose!

We pulled into the station
at Two Forks River Bend.
Twain One grabbed his suitcase,
Twain Two his French hens.
I stood there despondent,
waving at my new friends.
Twains leaving this train,
would I see them again?

Now it's many years later,
I'm long in the tooth,
In line with my boy,
Our first flight to Duluth!
Then he turns with a gasp,
"Oh, how very uncouth!
"Two Twains on this plane,
with Italian Vermouth!"

The Wall

Paul Lonardo

"Hey, everyone," Ray Ray howled in delight, "look what I found!"

Leslie screamed and ran off when she saw the matted calico fur and stiff body of the lifeless cat Ray Ray was holding up by its tail. Her terror amused the freckled-faced boy, who bounded after her, bellowing excited, deranged laughter. His hair was so red that in the scorching Maryland sun his head looked like it was on fire.

"Get it away," she shrieked.

"Don't worry, it can't hurt you," he assured her, sunlight spangling off his braces. "It's dead."

"Get it away, Ray Ray!" Leslie raced down the path and into the woods. She was too fast for her pursuer. Her fear of cats was redoubled by the state of decay this one was in.

Anthony, a heavyset, brooding boy, was sitting Indian-style in front of a high wall of granite stone blocks a short distance away. He had turned over a long, flat stone and was inspecting a strange red bug he had corralled in the palm of his hand. He didn't look up as Ray Ray sat down across from him and set the decomposing animal on the ground between them. Unflinchingly, he touched a finger to one unseeing eye. He thought it would feel like a marble, but it felt more like a SuperBall.

Nearby, little Paulie was crouched in a thicket dominated by milkweed, peeling the pointy pods open to release the downy-tufted seeds inside. Seeing Ray Ray, he jumped up, wiping the white juice from the plant on his jeans.

Ray Ray's braces flashed as he looked up at Paulie and smiled. "It's got all maggots in its belly," he marveled.

"What do you think it did wrong?" Paulie asked quizzically.

"Maybe it scratched a little girl all up when it was a kitten," Ray Ray suggested, after thinking about it for a moment.

Anthony pressed his thumb into the palm of his hand, disintegrating the colorful bug. "You think that bug did anything wrong?" Being by far the biggest and strongest, he was the unchallenged leader of the group.

"Let's bury it," Paulie proposed.

Anthony stood, looking down dispassionately as Paulie and Ray Ray used pointed stones to break the callous topsoil. When they got down about six inches, they set the carcass into the hole and troweled the earth back over it with their hands.

Paulie jabbed the sharp edge of his stone into the soft dirt at the head of the shallow grave. It stood upright like a tombstone. He felt better now. He knew the others would make fun of him, so he abstained from shedding a tear. He had never seen the cat before, but he knew that somebody was going to miss it a lot. He recited a silent prayer to himself.

"I thought we were going to Doc's," Anthony interrupted, abruptly bringing the pet funeral to a close. "Come on."

When he turned and started down the path, Ray Ray whispered to Paulie, "Next month, we'll dig up the bones and bring them to Mr. Dresner's biology class when school starts." As he jogged off to catch up with Anthony, Paulie hesitated before kicking over the stone marker. Then he quickly retreated to join the others, walking with his head craned around, holding the spot with his eyes for as long as he could before losing it in the monotony of the landscape.

Farther along the path, Lenny was sitting beside Leslie in front of a stagnant, black-water pond, skipping stones across the surface and watching the water bugs scatter.

"Where are they?" Lenny asked. "I have to go to my cousin's house in a little while. It's his birthday."

"They'll be along." Leslie's words were measured and reassuring.

Lenny relaxed a little and looked at Leslie. She smiled at him and he turned away, flushing. He had begun feeling something he did not fully understand. He felt like he might be sick, but he was perfectly fine. He didn't know what caused it, but it only happened to him when Leslie was around, when he looked at her, the way her skin and auburn hair glowed in any light, the sound of her voice, and the way she moved and walked. Even the way she smelled. He felt different around her. He acted different, and he was hardly aware how he would make sure he brushed his teeth and combed his hair if he knew she was going to be around.

"Lenny-and-Leslie-sitting-in-a-tree," Anthony taunted from the edge of the path.

"K-I-S-S-I-N-G," Ray Ray and Paulie joined in. "First comes love, then comes marriage, then comes baby in a baby carriage." They broke off into fits of laughter, and as Anthony initiated another chorus, Lenny jumped up, red-faced, and struck out in pride's defense, pushing and shoving Anthony to get him to stop. Anthony instantly spun the smaller boy around, capturing him in an inescapable chokehold.

Unable to move, Lenny felt an angry and frustrated sob building up inside of him. He only hoped he could hold it off so Leslie wouldn't notice.

"What's the matter, lover-boy?" Anthony chided. "You going to cry in front of your girlfriend?"

Leslie stood up and marched down the path alone, hiding her own tears.

"Let go of me, you blimp," Lenny said, his voice tiny and strangled.

"Say, please, uncle Anthony."

"Please, Uncle Blimp."

"That's not it." Anthony squeezed tighter. His sizeable forearms pressed against Lenny's throat, making the boy gag and drop to his knees. "Say it."

"Okay, okay," Lenny wheezed. "Please, Uncle Anthony."

"What? I can't hear you."

"Please, Uncle Anthony. Now let go." He fell to the ground when he was released, rubbing his neck and coughing. He lay there for a moment in shame, his eyes wet, when Anthony suddenly reached down and offered his hand in atonement. Lenny took it and Anthony pulled him to his feet.

"You okay?" Anthony asked.

Lenny nodded and dried his eyes with the back of his hands. Anthony put an arm around Lenny's shoulder and the two of them started down the path together. Paulie and Ray Ray joined them and they all locked arms, forming a chorus line and goose-stepping out of the woods. In unison, they began chanting, "Anybody-in-the-way-gets-a-five-cent-kick-and-a-ten-cent-punch." They repeated this mantra until they emerged from an open field, the scent of lavender and heady chokecherry dancing in the breeze. They arrived at the intersection of two dusty roads and entered a small convenience store, Doc's, to buy their favorite candy.

On their way back home through the woods they dawdled in silence, chomping on Tootsie Rolls and gnawing on Jawbreakers. They were rounding a bend in the path when a boy they had never seen before appeared. A bright red whistle dangled from a yellow string around his neck. The five children gathered around him in a semi-circle.

"Can I play with you?" the boy asked. "My name is Johnny." He pronounced it *Jawnny*.

"You talk funny," Ray Ray informed the new boy.

"So do you," Johnny said.

"That's the way everyone 'round here talks," Anthony said gubernatorially.

"This is how everyone talks in Boston, where I come from."

"*Baw-stin*," Ray Ray mocked.

"*Tawks*," Paulie added.

They both laughed.

Johnny ignored them. "What do you got in the bags?" he asked.

"Candy," Leslie answered.

"I'll let you blow my whistle if you share with me."

The other children looked at each other deliberately. Ray Ray was the first one to dig into his bag and offer up a root beer barrel. Handed the lustrous whistle, he breathed in deeply to fill his lungs with as much air as they could stand, then blew mightily. It produced a loud, piercing trill that set birds to flight from the surrounding trees. Ray Ray brought the instrument to his lips a second time, but Johnny snatched it away from him.

"One candy, one turn," the new boy lectured. "Who's next?"

Anthony muscled passed Paulie, trading an Atomic Fireball for a tootle.

By the time everyone had several turns, Johnny had all their candy in his pockets.

"What's that?" the boy asked the other children, awed by the high wall of haphazardly stacked rocks. It zigzagged at precarious angles and extended out of sight into shadows under the canopy of trees in both directions. He had noticed it in the distance as he was walking, but this was the closest point that the meandering path strayed to the wall, and it was even more impressive up close, towering twenty feet overhead. Much too tall to see over. Walking right up to it, he put a hand against one of the large stone slabs near the bottom, expecting it to be cool to the touch, but it was surprisingly warm.

The other children remained on the path.

"What's on the other side?" Johnny wanted to know.

"Hell," Paulie said flatly.

The new boy looked back at them. "There's no such thing as Hell."

"We're Baptists," Leslie apprised the boy, "and we believe in Hell."

"My daddy's an atheist," Johnny boasted, "and he says Hell is just a make-believe place that was invented to put people in that you don't like." He turned back to the stone wall. "Seems sturdy enough to climb."

"Aren't you afraid of the Devil?" Ray Ray asked.

"Nope."

The others all gasped.

"I'm not afraid because there is no Devil," the boy continued. "That's why I wear this." He tugged on the yellow whistle string. "If anybody tries to hurt me or make me go somewhere with them that I don't want to go, I just blow on my whistle as hard as I can and keep blowing until my mommy or daddy come."

"What if they don't?" Anthony said, more like a warning.

"They will." Johnny put one foot up on a ledge between two stones, about six inches off the ground, and was about to start climbing when a fetid odor wafted over the wall. He stopped suddenly, wrinkling his nose in disgust. Mingled with the scent of lavender, the stench was cloying. "Do you smell that?"

The other children looked at each other before Lenny spoke up. "That's the smell of burning flesh in a lake of fire, where doomed souls go around and around forever."

Johnny looked back at them. "How do you know? Have anyone of you ever seen that?"

"We don't have to see it," Ray Ray reported. "We just know it's there."

"You can't know anything without proof."

"Don't you believe in mysteries, either?" Leslie probed.

"Sure, but once you find the truth it's not a mystery anymore. The Devil isn't real. And neither is Hell." Johnny turned his attention back to the wall and how he was going to scale it.

"You can make things real if you believe hard enough," Anthony told him.

"Smells like a swamp," Johnny concluded. "That's what it is."

"How do you know *that*?" Paulie challenged the boy.

"I know," Johnny said with conviction as he secured a handhold and hoisted himself off the ground. "My daddy is a colonel in the army. He works at the Aberdeen Proving Ground, that's why we moved here. The military put up this wall to keep people from seeing what they're doing. That's Swan Creek on the other side. Probably got them big snapping turtles in there. I bet one of them died, and that's what smells." He clung to the wall a moment before he started ascending upward with ease. Reaching the top, he swung one leg over and then the other. He sat there a moment smiling as he peered out at the grand vista, then turned to his new friends and shouted, "See, I told you. Just a big old smelly swamp. Nothing to be afraid of. I'm going over."

"Once you cross over, you can't come back," Lenny reported.

Johnny just waved, then he disappeared over the edge on the other side of the wall.

Several moments later came the far-off sound of a bright red whistle on a yellow string. Once. Twice. Three times. The last one persisted for several seconds, then it slowly died away.

Ray Ray looked over at Paulie and said, "I didn't like him."

When Anthony turned and started up the path, the others followed naturally. Paulie hesitated, and when the others turned their backs on the wall he reached down and picked up the largest stone he could carry and secured it into place near the bottom of the wall. As he walked away, he tried to keep his eye on the Johnny's stone for as long as he could.

The children followed the path out of the woods on their way home, the redolence of lavender and sulphur heavy in the air.

The Test

Hank Ellis

As Peter dragged his exhausted body out of the mud, he noticed movement in the shrubs along the edge of the forest. Unsure of what it might be, he picked up two large rocks and a heavy stick for protection. With his back up against a large boulder, he sat and stared at the bushes. The short rest was welcomed because it gave his weary body some time to recover. *Whatever it was, it's gone*, he thought. But just to make sure, he tossed his stick into the shrubs. A thud was followed by a low-pitched groan.

"Is there someone in there?" He waited another ten seconds. "Come out, or I'm going to throw this rock in there." But nothing happened! "Okay, I warned you." Mustering up what little strength he had left, he stood in front of the boulder and reared back to toss his rock. Before he let go, a young native boy poked his head above the shrubs. The two boys looked at one another until Peter finally succumbed to his injuries. Cut, bruised, out of breath, and totally exhausted, the apprentice caretaker collapsed in the sand.

It could have been hours or even days before Peter finally opened his eyes. He found himself lying in a cloth hammock staring at a thatched roof. Green bananas, gourds, and clay pots were hanging from vine-like ropes in the ceiling. The walls of the dwelling were made of wood, bamboo, and reeds and the floor was dirt. He noticed that someone had put ointment on his cuts. As his head turned to view the remainder of the room his eyes stopped at the doorway. Three young children were staring at him. Peter smiled. "How are you guys?" The kids giggled and moved away from the door. Thirty seconds later a middle-aged woman walked through the doorway with the same boy he had encountered along the river. "Hello," said Peter.

"Olá, como você está se sentindo?" was the woman's reply.

He had never heard such words, but he understood what she was saying. "Did you just say hello, how are you feeling?"

"Yes, of course."

"Do you understand me?" asked the surprised boy.

"Of course! You speak our language very well."

Peter couldn't imagine how they could understand each other until he remembered the sound of the wind and the poachers in Africa. Eli's touch had allowed him to make sense of the African language. *I guess it works everywhere*, he thought.

Rising from the hammock, the recovering boy introduced himself. "My name is Peter. Thank you for helping me."

"You are very welcome, Peter. My name is Manoela and this is my son Jordao. He has told us much about you."

Peter was puzzled by her statement. "What did he tell you?"

"He says you command the Boitata. And you throw very well," she said with a laugh.

It took Peter several seconds to understand why she was laughing, but when he glanced at Jordao he remembered. "Oh—I'm sorry Jordao. Are you okay? I didn't know what was hiding in the bushes."

"I am fine," answered the young boy. "I was more surprised than hurt. It is good to see that you are doing well."

"So tell me," asked Manoela, "is it true?"

"Is what true?" replied the puzzled boy.

"That you command the Boitata."

"What is the Boitata?"

"It's the huge fire-snake that lives on the river. It is the protector of the forests, meadows, and jungle. Jordao told the village that you rode its back and that you talked to it."

Peter's mind raced. *How can I explain this*? he thought. *I wish Paloma was here.* The longer he thought about it, the more anxious he became. He finally blurted out the truth as he knew it. "There was a big fire. I fell in the river and drifted in the current. I was about to go over the waterfall and I felt something below me—so I grabbed it. It was a large snake that took me to the shore. I don't know if that was Boitata, but I was very thankful. That is all I know."

Manoela looked at Jordao to check on the accuracy of the story. "Is this true?"

"Yes, there was a large fire on the other side of the river. But I did not see this boy until he was two hundred yards from the waterfall. He grabbed Boitata and spoke to him at the shoreline. Boitata stared at the boy for a moment and then moved away. What he says is true."

Manoela wasn't sure what to do with this story. It was already traveling throughout the village. But she didn't have to think about it long because a grizzled old man burst into the dwelling.

"Show me this white-boy who commands the Boitata," spoke the intruder.

Peter assumed the ill-mannered person was the chief of the village, because Manoela and Jordao lowered their heads at his entrance. *"Chefe!"* called out Manoela, "please meet our guest Peter."

Despite the discourteous intrusion into Manoela's home, Peter also bowed as a sign of respect to the elderly man.

"So, you command the Boitata!"

"Ah, no sir. A snake saved me, but I didn't command it."

"I have never heard of such a thing. Why would a snake save you? They would rather eat you than save you. And all this happening during a forest fire? That is when the Boitata shows up. Did you start the fire?"

"Oh no, sir, I am very careful with fire. I was running toward the river because I had no other place to go."

Everyone in the room watched the old man as he pondered the situation. Eventually, he glanced at Manoela and asked if the boy had eaten.

"No chief, he just woke up. I'm sure he is very hungry." Peter nodded as she glanced in his direction.

"Then feed him well and get him strong. Remember, tomorrow is the village feast and celebration. We will let the village decide."

"What will they decide?" asked Peter.

"You will see," he mumbled as he headed out the door.

"Manoela, do you know what he meant?"

"I'm sorry, Peter, but I don't. He is very impulsive. Sometimes he worries me. But right now, let me get you something to eat. You must be very hungry."

"Thank you—I am. How long have I been here?"

"Jordao and some men from the village brought you here yesterday. You have been sleeping ever since."

After a delicious meal of fresh-cooked fish and sweet potatoes, Jordao showed Peter the village.

The blonde-haired white boy, paired with the black-haired olive-skinned boy, were a sight to behold as they walked through the village. They were about the same height with the same lanky muscular build—both taller than most boys their age. As they eyed the huge hut in the center of the village, Jordao explained that this was where the festival would be held. Several girls were helping to prepare the hut for the ceremony.

"Hello Jordao," said one of the girls. "How are you today?"

"Hi Catia, I'm doing well. How are you?"

"I am fine. I talked to your mother and she tells me that tomorrow is a big day for you—a birthday and your first test. That is amazing."

Peter's eyes widened and a big smile filled his face as soon as Catia finished. "Your birthday is tomorrow?" he asked.

"Yes, why all the excitement?"

"It is also my birthday. I will be thirteen."

Jordao's face beamed. "It is? That's incredible!"

"Excuse me, Jordao. Who is this boy?" asked Catia.

"I'm sorry—this is my friend Peter. Peter, this is Catia."

The pretty young girl smiled at the village newcomer. "Hello Peter, it is a pleasure to meet you. Are the stories true?"

By now, Peter understood that many "stories" were being passed around the village, but he was curious to hear what this beautiful young girl had heard. "I don't know. What are the stories?" he asked.

"That you have amazing powers and that you command the Great Boitata."

"All I can tell you is that I was about to go over the waterfall. I felt something beneath me. I grabbed on, and it took me to the shore. I don't know why it saved me, but I was glad and said thanks."

"Well, no matter what the stories, you must be very special for it to save you. Will you be going to the festival tomorrow?"

"Ah, ah—I guess," he stammered. This was the first time since waking that he thought about a future event. Manoela, Jordao, the Chief, and now Catia had been asking him questions constantly. As he wondered about tomorrow he became worried about David and the caretakers. *They must be going crazy looking for me*, he thought. But the more he thought about Catia's question, he realized there was only one answer. Jordao had rescued him after his collapse and had referred to him as his friend several times when speaking with the villagers. Peter was honored. The least he could do was attend the celebration. "I meant to say, I'd consider it a privilege. Maybe I'll see you tomorrow," replied Peter.

"I'll look forward to it," answered the smiling girl.

As Peter and Jordao left the area Peter asked if Catia was his girlfriend. Jordao laughed. "No, she is a good friend—one I have known all my life, but she is not my girlfriend. Why? Do you like her?" teased Jordao.

"She's nice—why don't you tell me about the festival?" asked Peter, quickly changing the subject.

Jordao explained that the entire village celebrates the summer's harvest with a great feast. It is followed by the test of manhood. As Jordao talked, Peter began thinking about what marked manhood back home. He had never thought about it before. It would be a great question for his dad, mom, Eli, or any of the caretakers. But the thought of putting your hands into gloves filled with bullet ants was horrendous and fascinating at the same time. Peter couldn't resist asking about the nature of the test.

"Jordao, how do they get the ants into the gloves? Wouldn't they all run out?"

"No, Peter, the ants are sedated by the medicine man. Then hundreds of them are weaved into reed gloves with their stingers facing into the glove. Their narrow waists keep them in place. When the ants awaken they can't get out. Another reed glove is placed over the bullet ant glove," answered Jordao. "Why all the questions?"

Peter had been thinking about it ever since he learned that Jordao would be tested at the festival. "I want to test with you."

Jordao stared in disbelief. "Why would you do such a thing? You have nothing to prove. Someone who rides the Boitata does not need to prove he is a man. And you are not from this village. I'm not sure they will let you participate. I would be honored to have you join me in this test, but why subject yourself to such incredible pain?"

Peter began to reconsider his declaration the more Jordao spoke. "I'm not sure I understand why, Jordao, but I think I want to do this. I will sleep on my thoughts and if I still want to join you tomorrow, I will ask the Chief at the feast."

"Very well, Peter—whatever your decision, you are a good friend."

That night Manoela prepared a feast fit for kings and queens. She knew that the birthday celebrations of the two boys might get overlooked in the festival. And she also knew that Jordao would be in excruciating pain later in the day. This was her time to wish her son a happy birthday. Much to Peter's delight, she invited Catia and several of her friends to join the party. Peter got to meet Jordao's younger sisters and he learned that his new friend had lost his father only two years ago. It was a time to eat, talk, share the sad times, and celebrate new friendships.

But all too soon it was time for bed. The guests left the hut and the family cleaned up for the night. Peter returned to his makeshift hammock and Jordao extinguished the lit candles.

"Jordao!" whispered Peter.

"Yes, Peter. What is it?"

"Thank you for helping me. I think you are already a man. I know you will do well tomorrow."

"Thank you, my good friend. That means a lot coming from you."

"We all know he will do well tomorrow," came a voice from across the room. "Now go to sleep so he will be well rested," whispered Manoela.

Decision

Whether it was the food, the new surroundings, talk during dinner, or the underlying fear of tomorrow's test, Peter had difficulty sleeping. Many scenarios of him and the bullet ants played out in his head. It wasn't until the darkest part of the night that he finally fell asleep. But it didn't last long. He felt someone tug at his arm and whisper in his ear. "Peter, get up and come outside."

"Jordao, is that you?" he whispered back.

"Shh," the voice whispered. "Do not say anything."

Peter turned to view the intruder pulling on his arm, but couldn't see anything. "Who is there?"

Before he had a chance to say any more, Peter heard the words "come outside." But this time the words were in his thoughts, not his ears. Now knowing who it must be, he rose from his hammock and started for the door.

"Peter, are you okay?" whispered Jordao.

"I'm fine, I'll be right back. Go to sleep."

Safely outside and in the darkness of night Eli materialized in front of the lost boy. "I knew it must be you," smiled Peter as he hugged the giant guardian.

"I'm glad you are doing well," answered Eli. "It seems you have found a temporary home with these fine folks."

"They have been wonderful. I feel like I have another brother. And speaking of brothers—I hope David is safe."

"He is well and anxious to see you. Are you ready to leave?"

"Oh Eli, I can't leave now. Jordao saved me, his mother has been feeding me, and tomorrow is his test to become a man. Did you know we both turn thirteen tomorrow?"

Eli smiled, "Tell me Peter, what's really going on?"

"I would like to stay a little longer to support Jordao. And I think…I want to become a man as well. But I'm afraid!"

"Oh Peter, you are such a joy. Your desire to support and comfort your friend demonstrates your own developing manhood. But please know that the measure of a man is not the amount of pain he can withstand. And it has little to do with his age. Physical changes in a boy are not signs of manhood. It goes well beyond puberty and hormones. Compassion, serving others, always being there, and remaining humble in the face of acclaim are all marks of manhood. Just ask any of the caretakers—men or women. They will tell you the same thing.

"But why does Jordao have to go through this horrible test?" asked Peter.

"Because these practices are passed on from generation to generation. This same practice was ongoing hundreds of years ago when boys needed to be toughened in order to survive. Preparing for war, accidents, catastrophe, and other hardships, the boys were made tough for the sake of the tribe. Eventually, this practice will end. But unfortunately for Jordao it is still ingrained in the culture."

"Eli, I can already see many marks of manhood in Jordao. Ever since his dad died, he has become a greater help to his mother and sisters. And he spoke up when some older boys were mocking me."

"It sounds to me like he's already there," said Eli. "So tell me—why do you want to test yourself?"

Peter looked into the eyes of wisdom for several seconds. "To see if I can do it."

"Is that the only reason?"

"And to support Jordao. But don't ask me which is more important."

"I won't, but I think you already know the answer to that question."

As Peter contemplated Eli's statement, he surprised the master guardian with another question. "Eli, is there anything I can do to pass the test without much pain?"

"Yes, of course, but you will never know if you were able to pass Jordao's test if I tell you."

"I understand. Then I will take my chances without your help."

"And I understand as well," said Eli. "Please know that many of us, including your brother, will be watching the test when it is your time."

Peter was overjoyed to hear Eli's declaration. "Thank you, Eli—for everything," replied the teary-eyed boy. "Would you say hi to David. I miss him already."

"I will tell him. Before I leave, I have one final request—three mornings from now I want you to go to the river and wait. Can you do that?"

"Yes sir, but I don't know the way. I will need Jordao to take me. Is that okay?"

"That will be fine. It's time for me to go. The apprentice and master caretaker hugged each other and Eli was on his way.

The Test

Peter had a restful sleep through the remainder of the night. He woke to the eyes of Jordao's three-year-old sister Elisabete, staring in his face.

"Well, hello," said the startled boy. "How are you this morning?"

The little girl didn't answer, she just continued to stare. Her gaze was penetrating—seeking the innermost being within this strange white boy who was invited into her home by her mother and brother. Peter began to feel like she knew his deepest secrets as she continued her search. "Who was the man with you?" asked Elisabete.

Peter's smiling face changed to a look of concern while a myriad of questions ran through his mind. *Kids say the craziest things. Maybe she's thinking about something that happened yesterday or maybe she has a vivid imagination.* Quickly regaining his composure, he asked, "What man?"

"The very big and old man," she replied.

Peter's look of concern returned. *How could she see him?* he thought. *Eli was invisible.* "Um, ah, I'm not sure what man you are ..."

"Elisabete! Stop bothering Peter," instructed Manoela. "He has a big day today. I'm sure he will answer your questions later. Come over here, I need your help."

As the little girl turned toward her mother, Peter breathed a sigh of relief. *That was close!*

"Peter, would you like some breakfast?" asked Manoela.

Before he had a chance to respond, Jordao whispered in his ear. "All of the boys taking the test for manhood do not eat during the day. It is part of the preparation. If you still want to take the test, we should speak to the chief immediately."

"I do," he whispered. "Let's find him."

While readying themselves for their talk with the chief, Peter thanked Jordao's mom for the offer of breakfast, but told her he wouldn't be needing it. Despite Peter's whispers to her son, Manoela knew exactly what was going on. She was delighted that this kind stranger would make such a sacrifice to support Jordao.

The chief also was delighted that Peter would participate in the test. The tribe elder had felt pressured to address all of the magical stories that surrounded the young stranger. He had intended to ask the village at the festival whether the white boy who commands the Boitata should participate in the test for manhood or be declared a man because of his great abilities. He was sure the village would demand that the stranger take the test because none of them, except Jordao, had seen his incredible feat. But because of Peter's willingness, the chief no longer needed to ask the question.

With the exception of ten boys, the feast was enjoyed by the entire village. Jordao, Peter, and eight other boys were preparing themselves for the evening ritual. In previous festivals, six of the boys had already undergone one or more of the agonizing tests. Jordao, Peter, and two others were first-timers. Under the guidance of the elders, each boy wore the paint of his choice, usually black lines and symbols. Their backs, chests, and faces were decorated in the fashion of a warrior. The boys repeating the test were given special markings. Animal bones, feathers, or special paint was worn to show how many times they had passed their test. Some of the boys wore headbands. Several of the elders and some of the women took turns painting Peter. When one of the elders painted the symbol of a snake on his back, some of the other painters began to argue. The chief was called in to resolve the issue.

"Chief, this is a strange white boy, yet Fernao wants to paint the great snake on him," protested one of the elders. "I do not think it is right." Peter's light complexion was a stark contrast to some of the paints they chose and the Boitata—the figure representing the snake of fire—would be clearly visible to the entire village.

"Valerio, leave the symbol on the boy," answered the chief. "The stories in the village will either be confirmed or challenged depending on how the boy does. After all, shouldn't someone able to command the Boitata be able to pass the test of manhood? We will let the ants decide if he is worthy of the stories."

The more the older men spoke of such things, the more Peter questioned his decision. Broken bones, cuts, bruises, migraine headaches, the flu, stings from red ants, hornets, bees, and yellow jackets were all painful experiences he had endured during his childhood, but the stories of this test were renowned. Could he withstand the pain? He didn't know. And it was too late to back out now.

The time was finally here—something that Jordao had imagined ever since he witnessed the test nine years earlier. An older boy named Emilio was the first to participate. With village onlookers chanting a common song, he stepped forward to the wooden railing in the middle of the huge hut. The recently awakened bullet ants, already woven into the reed gloves, were placed into larger woven gloves. Emilio placed his elbows on the wooden railing and set his arms in an upright position as the elders slowly moved the gloves over his outstretched hands. The people by his side held his arms gently while some elders, women, friends, and family danced to the village song. It was incredible to watch. Clearly, he was experiencing agonizing pain yet his face remained focused.

Peter wondered where he went. Did his mind leave his burdened body? Did he simply grit his teeth and bear the pain? He wondered these thoughts and many more as he watched each of the previously tested candidates experience five minutes in the gloves filled with bullet ants. It was now Jordao's turn. As Peter moved to the railing with his new-found friend, he heard a voice in his head. The apprentice caretaker was becoming accustomed to this magical voice. "Peter, we are here. Tell Jordao to focus on his family and to remember his father. He should do well," said the voice.

Holding his arm, Peter whispered Eli's instructions to his brave friend.

Jordao whispered back "Thank you, Peter," as they placed the gloves over his hands.

Jordao had previously experienced the sting of a bullet ant. In fact, most of the people in the tribe had been stung sometime in their lives. But to intentionally expose yourself to hundreds of stings seemed crazy to Peter. All he could do was hold his friend's arm and dance with the village. Jordao was exceptional. The pain was in his face but he took it like a seasoned warrior. After five minutes they took the gloves off. Already, Jordao's hands were bent, swollen, and paralyzed. Sweat glistened on his olive skin as he walked around in circles. Peter had to let him go because it was his turn to face the ants and his fears.

But it was an odd thing to watch when Jordao forced himself back to Peter's side. Clearly he was in agonizing pain, yet he wanted to be there. Although his hands could not feel to grip, Jordao inserted himself between Peter and his closest supporter. He pushed his left stump of a hand around Peter's right elbow and danced with everyone else. The young white boy acknowledged his companion's support, but was too preoccupied to smile. He raised his hands for the gloves and the pain began. Since he had never been shot, he couldn't understand the reference to the pain of a bullet. His only comparison was the sting of yellow jackets or slamming your fingers in a door. He even remembered the time a wooden splinter traveled halfway up his fingernail. But these thoughts were fleeting because his new reference for pain was incredible. This test gave new meaning to the doctor's pain assessment scale where a ten was unimaginable and unspeakable. As his mind raced, he could see some familiar faces along the back wall of the hut. Eli, Gabrielle, Paloma, Sierra, Anastasia, and David were watching him—at least he thought they were. During a few moments of imagined clarity, he knew they couldn't be there. As the gloves were removed, Peter's face and the whites of his eyes reddened to a point that frightened some of the villagers. Perhaps this was the boy who commands the fire snake?

An hour later, the boys were in more pain than ever. It was important that someone from the tribe oversee each boy. Jordao and Peter were watched continually by Catia, Catia's friends, and Manoela. Several of the boys, including Peter, began to hallucinate. The white wonder, as many of the villagers called him, began to jump in the air as if he could fly, then he would walk into walls thinking he was invisible. When he started to cry out "Eli! the pain is incredible," the tribe became concerned. "Who is he calling?" asked the chief.

Eli also was concerned that he may inadvertently reveal the existence of the caretakers to the entire village. He hesitated, but eventually answered the hurting boy. "Peter, you will soon be fine. Think of David and your family. Know that the pain will pass!"

"But when will it pass, Eli?" shouted the hurting boy.

"Peter, when will what pass and who is Eli?" asked Catia in a gentle tone.

"The pain!" yelled the impatient and unrestrained boy. "And Eli is the guardian!" He continued his ranting for another minute before running into the rear wall of the building as if he were going to hug someone.

Catia was alarmed at Peter's loud and abusive reply and stopped her questioning. Manoela helped her understand that this was not the boy they had come to know. His pain and hallucinations were driving his erratic behavior.

As newcomers to the test, both boys endured the pain remarkably well. The hallucinations continued for hours, but neither boy passed out, nor did they cry. The overseers watched them through their sleepless night until the pain finally began to subside the following afternoon.

"Is it you?" asked Catia.

"It's me! I hope I didn't do anything crazy last night," answered Peter. "I remember very little after they took the gloves off."

"You were yelling at me a lot—about someone named Eli. Who is he?"

"Oh Catia, I'm so sorry. Please forgive me. I was not myself."

The young lady moved close to the apologetic boy, placed her arms around his neck and kissed him on the cheek. "Thank you, Peter, I know it wasn't you."

Peter was taken aback, but not disappointed, by Catia's action. His complexion, still red from the test, disguised his blushing face. Quickly refocusing, he asked how Jordao was doing.

"He's fine," smiled Catia. "His hands are still swollen and bent, but he did well. Let's go talk to him."

Jordao was resting on a stool outside the large hut when Catia approached. "Look who's with me!" she exclaimed. As he rose from his seat, Peter rushed forward and both boys embraced. Jordao was the first to speak. "You passed the test, my brother!"

"I did! And you did as well, my friend. How are you feeling?"

"Other than these useless hands, I feel like a different person. What about you?"

"I feel the same way, but I guess I lost my mind a bit last night," said Peter as he winced at Catia.

"I think we all did," said Jordao. "I'm so glad we both passed.

My Secret

Barbara Ann Whitman

I wish I were an artist;
I'd draw you in my world
With charcoal pencil flourishes
and lines that twist and swirl.
I'd kiss you on a rocky bluff
the sea churning below.
I'd ink my heart on yours
so you would finally know

That if I were a writer,
this story could be told:
Leather bound eternity
with pages rimmed in gold.
My pen would spell out how I feel
with words of dark desire.
The world would know how my heart burns
for you, a raging fire.

And if I were a minstrel,
a ballad I would sing:
A melody as bittersweet
as the tear that it would bring.
The lyrics would enfold you
and by the last refrain,
You'd be mine - at last, I'd know
I hadn't loved in vain.

I long to be a dancer

whose lyrical pliés
would move you so, there'd be no doubt;
you'd love me all your days.
My gestures would bewitch you
as you'd struggle not to cry.
I'd hold you close and slow dance
beneath a starry sky.

Alas, in sorrow, I confess
that I am just a schemer.
The only talent I possess
is that of lonely dreamer.
You'll never understand
the weight and depth of my regret.
My love for you will die with me
and always be my secret.

The Boy at the Window

Anne-Marie Sutton

The stern face of President William McKinley gazes down on the pupils of Miss Harriet Archer's classroom. President McKinley, elected in 1896, has been in office four years, and his picture hangs in every American schoolroom. The flag displayed next to his image has forty-five stars representing the country's forty-five states, Utah the last state admitted to the union.

Harriet Archer, the founder of the Chesterfield School for Girls, stands at the head of the class. The cast-iron potbelly stove is unlit as it is early September and the room is warm. A large clock with a swinging pendulum tells the time. On the teacher's high wooden desk is a heavy brass bell and a hickory switch. The sound of the ringing bell is to summon Miss Archer's pupils. The wooden stick can be used when direct action is needed on misbehaving children.

The spacious schoolroom contains fourteen desks of varying sizes. The small desks at the front accommodate the five youngest girls, ages six and seven. Larger desks in the middle are for the five students aged eight to ten years old. Four girls ages eleven and twelve sit at the back of the room.

Among the older girls is a new pupil, Victoria Redstone. Her father's occupation as a <u>tinker,</u> a tinsmith who mends household utensils, has caused the family to move frequently during her short life. In June, Thomas Redstone had decided that the prosperous town of Chesterfield, Rhode Island offered greater opportunity than their native Connecticut and so the family moved once more.

Vicky is unhappy in her new Rhode Island home. She misses her old school, her friends, and the comfort of familiar surroundings. The three classmates of her own age at Miss Archer's school have made no attempt to offer friendship. Rebecca, Clara, and Annie enjoy rejecting Vicky, whispering and laughing with what the newcomer knows are criticisms of her looks, her clothes, and her efforts in class. More than once has Vicky felt the sting of hot tears in her eyes as she struggled to pretend not to notice their taunts and disapproval. At recess, she sits by herself in the garden, hidden away from her teasing peers.

The Chesterfield School is located in Miss Archer's own residence. The house's colonial style suggests that it was built around 1680. The original structure contained four rooms, a design known as a two over two, meaning that there were two living rooms downstairs and two sleeping rooms upstairs, all heated by a central chimney. The kitchen was located outdoors in a <u>lean-to</u> resting against the back wall of the house. When the home was enlarged in the late 1700s, the kitchen was moved inside to a hearth room with a large fireplace for cooking. It was in 1894 that the schoolroom was built onto the house to fulfill Harriet Archer's desire to start her own school for girls.

Harriet Archer is unmarried, and at the age of thirty-eight is likely to remain so for the rest of her life. She lives with her brother Joshua, a successful ship builder. Joshua's wife's premature death brought Harriet to keep house for her sibling. To reward her devotion, Joshua approved the addition of the school. He and his wife had no children of their own, and it pleases him to welcome the students into his home.

* * *

Today the lesson is on ancient Egypt. The younger girls are kept busy drawing pyramids. The middle group of girls are copying hieroglyphics from the blackboard. In the back of the room the older girls are composing essays on how mummies were preserved.

When the children take their break for lunch, Vicky eats her food quickly so that she can escape outside. The Archer house has a well-manicured garden with trees and benches and a wishing well. Vicky has a favorite secluded spot behind some bushes where she can sit unnoticed. Today as she walks across the grass she sees a shadow moving in one of the upstairs windows. Vicky tries to focus on the shape behind the glass. It is a small figure, perhaps that of a child. She frowns. Could it be one of the other students? Miss Archer does not allow the girls to go into the family living quarters.

When Vicky hears the bell calling the pupils back inside, she looks up at the window. The shadow is still there, and this time Vicky is sure what she is seeing is the silhouette of a boy about her own age. Without hesitation, she raises her hand to wave. The boy turns and stares at her. She is sure he can see her, but he makes no reciprocal greeting.

Back inside, at work on her essay, Vicky finds it hard to concentrate. Who is the boy upstairs? She had understood that the unmarried Miss Archer has no children. She knows from her parents' conversations that Joshua Archer's wife had died in childbirth, and the baby had died as well. She wishes she could ask one of the other girls what they know about this boy, but she is afraid that her questions will only bring more teasing.

* * *

No one was at the upstairs window when Vicky arrived for school the following day. She had come early to watch the window where she had seen the boy, but she was disappointed to see nobody there.

Once again her schoolwork failed to interest her. When Miss Archer asked her to recite her Latin homework, Vicky didn't answer.

"Victoria," Miss Archer said with a sharpness in her voice she usually reserved for the younger girls who had difficulty paying attention, "did you hear me call on you?"

Vicky stared at her teacher. "I am sorry, Miss Archer. What did you say?"

"I asked you to recite the passage you were to learn for your Latin homework. From the poem by Virgil." Miss Archer paused. "Why are you looking at me like that, Victoria? Are you feeling unwell, child?"

"Oh, no," Vicky answered quickly. "I was just thinking about the mummies."

"The mummies?"

"Yes, I was wondering if we would learn more about mummies today," she said, hoping she would be forgiven for telling the small white lie. She had been thinking about the boy in the window.

"Well," the teacher said, "I appreciate your interest in our history lesson. But first we must do our Latin exercise, Victoria."

"Yes, Miss Archer," Vicky said as she heard the muffled giggles from Annie and Clara on either side of her. She turned to see Rebecca rolling her eyes in amusement. "I am ready to recite."

"You may begin."

Vicky swallowed. Slowly and carefully she began.

"*Musa, mihi causas memora.*" (Translation: Muse, tell me the reason)

Miss Archer beamed her approval.

* * *

At the end of the school day, Miss Archer announced that she was going to the meeting of the St. Peter's Ladies Guild and needed the girls to hurry their departure so she could leave immediately for the church. Tea and cakes were served before the meetings started, and the teacher had often arrived too late to partake of the best selection of sweets. The chattering students, just as eager as their teacher to depart the school, hurriedly gathered their belongings. Vicky, eyeing the closed door leading to the family quarters, lingered behind the others. She wondered if the door was locked. Dare she try its handle?

Miss Archer, already wearing her hat, stood on the path outside as her pupils exited. When the older woman began putting on her gloves, her eyes focused on her hands, Vicky saw her chance. She reached for the door knob. It turned.

* * *

The interior of the house was dark. Heavy curtains were pulled across the windows. Vicky stood for several seconds in a room dominated by a big stone fireplace stacked with wood. A large black iron kettle hung from a hook. There was a long rectangular trestle table in the center of the room covered with pans and bowls and cooking utensils of the kind her father repaired.

Vicky's eyes soon adjusted to the dimness, and she could make out a winding staircase in the corner of the room. Taking a breath, her heart pounding, she began to climb its narrow wooden treads.

At the top of the stairway was a landing facing three closed doors. Vicky carefully opened the door on her left to a bedroom with a definite masculine air. She supposed this room belonged to Miss Archer's brother. Next she tried the middle door. This room had the light, delicate design of a woman's chamber. Although the girl was curious about her teacher's life, she had no time to look inside. She turned to the last door.

Inside the third room the curtains on the two windows were open, letting in the rays of the afternoon sun. Between the windows hung a somber portrait of a woman wearing an old-fashioned bonnet and a black dress trimmed in white lace. Her lips were shut tight in disappointment.

A four poster bed was covered by a thick blue and white quilt.

"Hello," she said softly to the shape beneath the quilt.

The figure in the bed stirred.

"Hello," she repeated, her voice louder. The boy in the bed, for now she could see the figure was a boy, moved his head slightly on the pillow. His face was thin, his skin pallid. Curling wisps of light brown hair framed his face.

"I'm Vicky," she said, approaching the bed.

The boy drew one of his hands from beneath the quilt. The long bony fingers moved slowly toward his throat, and he began to cough. Vicky lurched forward.

"Are you all right?"

The coughing continued, along with a deep wheezing sound coming from his chest. Vicky looked around the room.

"Is there water? You need to drink some water."

There was none and Vicky, helpless, could only wait for the harsh sounds to subside. The boy slumped back against the pillow.

"What is your name?" Vicky asked.

"Timothy Stokes," the boy answered in a soft whisper.

"Well, Timothy, I am pleased to make your acquaintance. I'm Vicky Redstone and I am a pupil in the school downstairs."

"I know."

"You do? How do you know that?"

"I see you from the window. You always sit alone in the garden."

"It was you I saw in the window the other day. I waved to you."

"You are lucky to be able to go to school." Timothy's voice was weak, and Vicky had to bend low to hear him. "I have never been allowed to go to school."

"Because you are sick?"

"I've always had to stay in bed," he said, choking on his words as his coughing began.

"You need to drink water. I can get you some," Vicky said. "There is a bucket in the schoolroom and a cup."

"No. I cannot drink water."

"You can't drink water? Everybody can drink water."

The coughing stopped and Timothy said, "I do so want to go to school someday."

"How do you learn your lessons?"

"My mother taught me. She read books to me and helped me to learn my numbers."

"Do you have to recite Latin?"

"No," the boy answered. "My mother never learned it."

"Who is your mother?"

"Mrs. Stokes, of course." He looked across the room at the portrait.

Vicky knew of no Mrs. Stokes in the neighborhood, but perhaps Timothy was visiting. "Is your mother in the house now?"

"No."

"So Miss Archer is taking care of you?"

"No."

Vicky sighed. She didn't understand everything that Timothy was saying, but she was beginning to be nervous that Miss Archer might return from the church and find her in the house.

"I had better be going back downstairs," she said. "Miss Archer doesn't know I came up to see you and, besides, the girls aren't allowed in the house. I have to go before she returns. I could be punished. But it was nice to meet you."

"Will you do something for me?"

"Yes. If I can."

"I have no books to read. Can you bring me a book to read?"

Vicky looked around the room. It was true, there were no books.

"We have geography books with maps and articles about the states and the countries of the world."

"I don't know much about geography."

"Of course, there are readers for the younger girls," Vicky added, not knowing how good his reading skills were, taught as he was by his mother who had never learned Latin and apparently never told him much about geography.

"Will you bring me the book with the maps? Timothy asked. "I would like to see the maps."

"Yes, Timothy. Next time I can come up to see you, I will bring you a geography book with maps."

* * *

Later that night Vicky lay in bed and thought about Timothy. How strange he had looked with his skin so pale and white that you could almost see through to his bones. She wondered what was the ailment that made him live his life in bed. And why couldn't he drink water? That was a most curious thing that he had said.

And where was the woman in the painting, the mysterious Mrs. Stokes?

With that last question in her thoughts, the girl drifted into sleep.

* * *

Several days passed and Vicky found no chance to visit Timothy again. Miss Archer remained in the classroom at the end of each school day, sitting at her desk reading the copy books filled with the children's work. There had been no sightings of her new friend in the window, and Vicky considered that perhaps Timothy no longer was in the house.

The geography books were kept on a high shelf and Vicky was confident that she could take one of them upstairs if only she had another opportunity to slip through the door into the living quarters while Miss Archer was away.

At last, on the following Monday, Miss Archer announced that she had another meeting to attend after school. When Amy Porter, one of the younger girls, bumped her knee and began to cry and Miss Archer hurried to her calm her, Vicky reached for one of the geography books and slipped it under her dress. With Amy settled, Miss Archer began to shepherd everyone out of the schoolroom. Vicky opened the door to the family quarters and hastened in.

How bold she was becoming, Vicky thought as she raced up the stairs before her presence was missed. She could only hope that Miss Archer would assume she had left with the older girls. At the top of the stairs Vicky didn't hesitate to open Timothy's bedroom door and enter without knocking.

He was asleep. At least the anxious girl hoped that he was sleeping. Timothy's face was so lacking in color and he lay so still that Vicky said a silent prayer that he was alive. For several seconds she stared down at his thin, unmoving form, afraid to speak his name for fear he was dead. At last she screwed up her courage and whispered his name. When there was no movement, she said his name louder.

"Timothy. Can you wake up? It's me, Vicky. I don't have a lot of time to visit today. I'm sorry I couldn't come sooner, but today was my first chance to come upstairs."

The shape under the quilt did not move, and Vicky reached out to touch him. His eyes flickered, and she drew her hand back. "Timothy, it's Vicky. Can you hear me?"

Timothy's eyes opened, and he gave an unsteady smile. "Have you brought my book?"

"Yes, oh yes," she said, relieved to hear his voice. She pulled the volume from beneath her skirt and put it on the bed. "How are you feeling today? I haven't seen you at the window."

"I'm tired," he said. "I tried to get out of bed but I couldn't."

"I can leave the book. I don't think Miss Archer will miss it. We haven't been studying geography for a while."

"Thank you."

"I wish you could come to school with me, even though you are a boy. You would learn so much. Miss Archer is a good teacher."

"Of course I want to go to a real school some day. Do you like history?"

"Yes," Vicky nodded.

"What are you learning about in history?"

"We were studying ancient Egypt. But we are finished with that now. Today our teacher taught us about the President because we have his picture in our schoolroom."

"What did she tell you about the war? My Uncle Robert is fighting in Virginia. I have been wondering if the North is winning."

"The North?" Vicky was puzzled. "Do you mean the North and South in the Civil War? We haven't studied the Civil War yet."

"But the President. You said you were learning about President Lincoln. You must be learning about the war, too."

"*President Lincoln!* Our class is studying President McKinley. *He* is the president." Didn't Timothy know anything?

The effort of speaking started the familiar wheezing in the boy's chest, the gasps followed by violent coughing. Vicky wished that she had been able to bring some water from the bucket.

When he finally stopped coughing, Timothy grew limp and closed his eyes. Vicky waited for several minutes, but when there was no further movement under the quilt, she crept quietly from the room.

* * *

Miss Archer greeted the girls as they came into school the next morning. Vicky stopped in front of her teacher.

"When was the Civil War, Miss Archer? Abraham Lincoln was president during the Civil War. Is that right?"

"Yes, Victoria. The Civil War started in 1861, the year when Mr. Lincoln became president. The South didn't want him to become president. They knew he was against slavery."

"Yes, and he freed the slaves. I learned about that in my last school. When did the war end?"

"It ended in 1865. Do you know that was also the year that President Lincoln was shot?" Vicky shook her head. "I was a little girl," Miss Archer continued. "When my mother told me that the President had died, I remember crying."

Vicky wanted to ask Miss Archer that if she was a little girl during the Civil War when Abraham Lincoln was the president, then did she know the boy upstairs who thinks that Lincoln is still the president? But it was so confusing because Miss Archer was now an adult, and Timothy was a child. She wondered if Timothy's illness has affected his mind. He had seemed like any other boy, albeit a sick one, when she first talked with him. Although what he said about not being able to drink water was still a strange thing which she could not figure out.

At the end of the school day, as the class was leaving, Vicky again approached Miss Archer.

"Miss Archer, how old is this house? It looks very old."

"The early history is undocumented, Victoria. It is generally accepted that it was built about 1680."

"Did you grow up here?"

"Oh, no. Our family lived in a house on Exeter Street. My father's ship building business was nearby."

"Oh," Vicky said. "I thought you might have lived here when you were a little girl during the Civil War and this was the house you lived in when you heard that President Lincoln died."

"No. I came here several years ago to live with my brother. He had purchased the house when he and Martha Jameson were married."

"Then your family has only lived here a short time."

"That is right. But before Mr. Archer bought this house in 1889 do you know it was lived in by the same family for more than one hundred years," she said proudly.

"A hundred years? Do you know the family's name?"

"Their name was Stokes."

* * *

"Timothy, how old are you?"

"Eleven."

"What year were you born?"

"1852."

"What year do you think it is now?"

"1863."

Once again Vicky had managed to reach Timothy's bedroom without Miss Archer's noticing her absence.

"1863," she repeated. "That was a long time ago." She counted in her head. "Thirty-seven years. But how... why," Vicky stammered.

"You might not believe me."

"Tell me," Vicky answered. "I want to know how it is possible that you can be born in 1852 and still look like a boy my own age."

"Because I died in 1863."

"Dead? You're dead? You can't be. You're here."

"Yes, I can be dead, Vicky. When I was eleven years old I died of consumption."

"You died?" She stared at him in amazement. "But that would mean... you're a ghost. You're a ghost? Wait a minute. Is that why you can't drink water?"

"Ghosts can't drink water. We don't eat food either."

"Do you like being a ghost?"

"No, I want to be with my parents in heaven where I won't be sick anymore."

"Why do you stay a ghost?"

95

"I really don't know the answer to that question. All I know is that after I died, I didn't leave this room."

"Didn't they bury your body?"

"Yes, my grave is in St. Peter's Church cemetery. But my spirit stayed here."

"But what about your mother and father? What did they do when they saw you in the bed?"

"My parents weren't able to see me even though I could see them. And when I tried to talk to them, they couldn't hear me."

"No one saw you?" Vicky asked. "Absolutely no one at all?"

Timothy shook his head.

"And they couldn't hear you coughing?" she asked skeptically.

"No."

"But I can," she pointed out.

"Yes, it's wonderful. When you waved to me from the garden I realized that you had seen me in the window. I was so happy. Then when you came to see me, you could see me... *and* hear me. You are the first person who has been able to do that."

"But why? After all these years?"

"I have been giving that some thought." The ghost of Timothy Stokes smiled. "I think it's because you needed a friend."

* * *

During the next several days Vicky continued to think about what Timothy had told her. She had never believed ghosts were real, just creatures you read about in stories. But now, not only had she met one but he had become her friend. And he wanted to go to school.

It was up to Vicky to make that wish possible. If no one could see him except for her, how could anyone know if he was in the classroom? His tiny figure could surely share her desk. Timothy would learn about history and geography, and even the Latin language.

The plan she devised was simple. She would get to school early in the morning and transport Timothy from his bedroom down the stairway to the schoolroom before the bell rang and the other girls came inside. Vicky was sure Timothy's ghostly body didn't weigh very much and she could help him walk. All that was needed was another distraction to Miss Archer's attention so the girl could get inside the residence.

It wasn't long before her opportunity came. A few days later, waiting in the garden before the bell rang, two girls started arguing and pulling each other's hair. Miss Archer heard their screams and rushed outside to separate them. Everyone - except for Vicky - crowded around the feuding girls.

* * *

Timothy was surprised to see Vicky so early in the day.

"I don't know if I can walk that far," he protested when he learned that she was there to take him downstairs.

"Of course you can. You can lean on me." He shook his head, but Vicky was determined. "Come on," she said in a strong voice. "We don't have much time." She turned the quilt back from his body. He was wearing a thin white nightshirt.

"Here, take my hand." Timothy put his hand in hers. His skin was dry and powdery, and she felt as if her fingers might go all the way through the tissue. But she grabbed his palm firmly and pulled. Timothy slowly began to rise from the bed. Vicky got him onto his feet and anchored to her shoulder.

"Can you take a step toward the door?"

With concentration, Timothy put his weight onto his feet and moved his left foot forward.

"Good," she encouraged him. "And now the right one. Keep walking."

Slowly they made it to the top of the stairs. "Put your hand on the railing," she commanded. "Take the steps one at a time. I'll hold on to you."

They reached the schoolroom door, and Vicky opened it a crack to look inside. A few girls were already at their desks, but she didn't see Miss Archer or the older students.

"This is it," she told Timothy.

An astonished Amy Porter, seeing Vicky come from inside Miss Archer's house, stared at her with wide eyes. Vicky gave her a conspiratorial smile and put a finger to her lips. Amy smiled back.

They were safe. They had made it. Timothy Stokes was going to school for the first time in his short life.

* * *

For Vicky, the hours of the school day seemed to fly by. First Miss Archer had the girls do their arithmetic. There were sums for the younger girls and multiplication for the older ones. Vicky worked on her problems, making sure that Timothy could see all her calculations.

Latin was next, and Vicky was thrilled that her new friend could witness her ability to recite Virgil's poems.

The history lesson was on the Spanish-American War which had been fought after William McKinley became President. Vicky saw Timothy concentrating hard to learn about this, the most recent war in American history. He listened closely as Miss Archer talked about the role played by Theodore Roosevelt, who had been a colonel who led a band of soldiers called the Rough Riders. They fought against the Spanish Army and won the famous battle of San Juan Hill in Cuba.

After history was finished, Miss Archer announced a short recess. The weather was pleasant, and she led the pupils outside to take some exercise. Vicky turned to Timothy.

"How do you like school so far?"

"It's wonderful," he said. "I cannot believe how much I learned already."

"I could see that you liked the Spanish-American War. I guess boys would like that stuff. Battles and soldiers and fighting."

"I liked Latin and arithmetic, too," he said.

"Timothy, what's wrong with you? You look strange," Vicky said. "I can see right through you now. I never could see through you before."

"I like being in school," Timothy said dreamily as his ghostly appearance began to fade.

Frantically Vicky reached for his arm. Her hand went right through his body.

"Thank you, Vicky, for bringing me to school with you. I'll never forget you."

"Timothy, wait," Vicky cried. "Don't leave. Please don't go."

But he was gone.

Now that Timothy Stokes had been able to go to school, his spirit had found peace at last.

The Sojourner

Judy Boss

Imagine a world where there is no time or space or material substance of any kind—a world where everything just is. Every so often this world intersects our world of time and space in the form of a sojourner. This is the story of one such sojourner who, although really nameless, we shall call Tobe.

Tobe was about to embark on a journey into time and space. Many had gone before him. Now it was his turn.

In order to prepare for the journey, he had to be separated off from the changeless Oneness. It felt strange at first, but Tobe soon got used to it. In a world of Oneness he could not really be separated from the inseparable. Separation was simply an illusion, necessary for making the journey. Knowing this gave Tobe comfort.

And now, at last it was happening. A vessel was available and Tobe had been assigned to it.

Though all sojourners eventually returned to the Oneness, since death, like time and space is an illusion, the journey was by no means without peril. The dangers of the time/space world were great and the price of failure or miscalculation high. Although the vessels or ships themselves were well-constructed and generally reliable, mishaps and even attacks from the outside were a looming threat and many sojourners perished in untimely and gruesome deaths before reaching their destinations. Those who did make it sometimes suffered from trauma or succumbed to one of the many diseases found in the world of time/space.

The planet to which Tobe's ship had been assigned was an especially dangerous and deceptive place. There was something hypnotic, almost numbing, about it. He had been warned that it was easy to get caught up in it and forget who you really were. Tobe was well aware of the dangers. But he also realized that, as an envoy of the Monarch, he could learn more and accomplish more there than at some of the safer destinations.

Those who had already made the journey cautioned Tobe. "Do be careful and don't forget us."

"Ooh, how exciting!" chimed in those who had not yet made the perilous journey, as they fluttered aside to let Tobe pass.

"Would anyone care to join me?" Tobe asked, peering into the vessel. "There's room for two in here—maybe even three."

There was a murmur from the crowd, but no one stepped forward.

"That's okay," Tobe said. "It will be more comfortable with just one. It is rather small after all."

While the Other whirled and resonated with wishes of good tidings, the mechanics busily hovered about making last-minute equipment adjustments.

The mechanics were a special class of servants who were able to travel instantaneously, without the need of a ship or time/space suit, between the world of the timelessness/formlessness and the world of time/space. This remarkable ability may give some readers the impression that they were a higher class of being—but not so. Their main task was to serve the sojourners by being on 24-hour call in case any of the sojourners should need assistance.

The majority of mechanics took great pride and delight in their work. However, they often complained, and understandably so, that if the sojourners would just take the time to put in a work order when trouble first arose there would be far fewer problems for both them and the sojourners.

Once, a long time ago, a few of the mechanics got huffy about their station in life. One of them even went so far as to go down to the world of time/space, where he stirred up a great deal of trouble. According to the latest reports, he is still at large, skulking about, getting into people's heads and making mischief wherever he could. He even had the audacity to falsely declare himself the real monarch to those gullible enough to believe him. Apparently he has amassed quite a following.

"Call whenever you need us," said the new chief mechanic as she checked Tobe's life support system one last time. "Remember, your communication device is built right into your time/space suit." She straightened up and pulled out a parchment and unrolled it for the umpteenth time. "It's very simple to use," she said, pointing to the diagram on the chart. "Use it whenever you need it—even if you just want to chat."

"I know," Tobe replied. How could anyone forget something so simple—so obvious? But of course he didn't say it out loud because he didn't want to hurt the chief mechanic's feelings. After all, she was just doing her job.

The chief mechanic scowled and tucked the chart back into a pocket under her wing. Everything was ready to go. Tobe waved goodbye to the enthusiast crowd.

"Don't forget us," the Other called after him. "Remember to stay in touch!" The air was alive with the fluttering of wings and tinkling songs of good wishes for a safe journey.

Tobe was deeply touched. "Of course I won't forget you," he answered. "How can I ever forget you?" And with those parting words he slipped into the awaiting ship.

At first it didn't feel very different. Tobe passed the time describing the new experience to the Other back home. The mechanics made periodic appearances. And just to keep them happy, Tobe made sure he put in a work order to the Monarch at the slightest sign of any problem.

For hours on end, when all was still, Tobe would lie back and listen to the soothing sound of the life support pump. Ka-thump, ka-thump. Tobe delighted in the rhythmic sound. It comforted him and sent nourishment surging through the lifeline to all parts of his new self. It was his lullaby in sleep and his companion when awake. The warm liquid in the time/space capsule pressed gently against his growing form. It was a strange, though not unpleasant, sensation as he floated though time/space to the alien world that would soon be his new home.

Sometimes the journey was so still and calm that Tobe wondered if the ship had come to a stop. At other times the ship lurched and jolted. But the liquid in the capsule cushioned him against harm.

Days passed, then weeks. Then, one day Tobe heard a second pump. At first, the sound was very faint. He wasn't even sure if he was really hearing it or just imagining it. But day after day, the sound grew stronger and stronger until he could hear it quite distinctly.

And so the two pumps—one slightly faster than the other—beat in harmony to create the new form—the time/space suit which would protect Tobe in the harsh environment on this alien planet.

The suit grew steadily larger, more complex, taking shape slowly and deliberately. He marveled at it, observed it, listened to it, touched it. The opportunities for education were endless. He reached up and touched his new facepiece. He felt his mouth. He had never had a mouth before. It felt good and soft and warm. He rejoiced in the new experiences, the new sensations.

Now, with so much going on around him and so much to learn, Tobe was kept busy. He still reported back, though less frequently than before. When all was quiet he would take time out from his education to communicate with the mechanics, to get last-minute instructions for his mission, and to chat with the Other back home. The communication device in his time/space suit was so simple to operate, he didn't know why the chief mechanic had made such a fuss about it.

One evening several months into his journey, the Monarch spoke to him. "Now rest up—you have a long and difficult job ahead of you. You will be landing soon. Take care and remember we will always be here for you."

"Remember to call us any time you need help," chimed in the chief mechanic in what sounded like a pre-recorded message. "Your communication device is built right into your time/space suit. I checked it over again and it's in perfect working order. Remember, it's very simple to operate. You just. . ."

Tobe tuned out the communication device. He smiled to himself. Yes, all was going well in this new world of time/space—so much to do, so much to learn. With that thought in mind he fell back into a peaceful sleep.

He was awakened a few hours later by an uncomfortable sensation. The ejection device had activated and was forcing him toward the hatch—pushing him, squeezing him. He tried to struggle. But it was no use. Tobe moved slowly toward the escape hatch, dragging his lifeline behind him.

Then—all of a sudden—he was out!

The shock was dreadful. The harsh glare hurt his new eyes. And it was cold—so cold. He felt naked—even in his time/space suit.

Suddenly a huge creature draped in pale green reached out and grabbed him. Tobe was terrified. Who were these strange alien creatures? The creature jerked him away from the time/space ship and slashed his lifeline.

Tobe felt numb with fear. How could he live without his lifeline? And where was the other pump? Surely this much be a malfunction—and the end for him. He struggled, gasping for breath. Then he felt a cold slap on his back. He let out a shriek of terror and fell back into semi-consciousness.

"It's a boy, Mrs. Hastings," the doctor said triumphantly. "A healthy eight pound, two ounce baby boy. Congratulations!"

The proud parents beamed down at their newborn son lying naked and dazed in the clear plastic bassinette beside the delivery table.

The Problem with Antiques

R. N. Chevalier

"Does it still work?" Jody asks the dealer at the flea market about the antique shortwave radio.

"Well, I don't rightly know," the old man answers. "But I got this box full of vacuum tubes, wires, a big antennae, and smaller things that go with it."

"How much?" she asks with wide-eyed curiosity.

"I'll tell ya what," the old man says with a sly smile. "Ten bucks and it's all yours." He squints as the August sunlight peeks past his umbrella, into his eyes.

"You've got a deal," she answers as she takes the money from her pocket. She trades the ten dollar bill for the old radio and big box of supplies.

"If ya don't mind me asking," the old man starts during the exchange. "Why is such a pretty young woman interested in such old equipment?"

"I'm curious about antique communications," she tells him. "I'm going to get this radio up and running as part of my college thesis."

"What are ya studyin'? If ya don't mind me askin'."

"Electrical engineering," she replies with a huge smile.

"Well, then." He smiles back. "Good luck to ya."

"Thanks," she says as she walks away.

She gets back to her small apartment and puts the items on the coffee table. She gets dinner ready. After she finishes eating, she cleans up.

Since tomorrow is Monday, all Jody wants to do is sit back and tinker with her new toy. She secures the antennae to the casing of the living room window, letting the bulky metal array protrude from the third floor window. She plugs the end of the antennae into the back of the radio, then plugs the radio's power cord into the wall outlet. She notices the time is eight o'clock.

Jody flips the power switch on. Nothing happens.

"Figures," she says to herself as she picks up the screwdriver from the table and begins to undo the screws holding the outer shell of the radio to the chassis. She takes the shell off, looking at the assortment of vacuum tubes.

"Okay, here we go," she says as she lights a blunt and begins to match the numbers on the darkened tubes to their new counterparts in the box. She replaces each tube in between puffs.

It's ten o'clock by the time she swaps out all the tubes. Jody sits back with a proud smile. She takes a final puff off the blunt and flips the power switch on again.

The *power on* light slowly brightens to life as the sound of static crackles through the speaker. The room glows in an eerie light, produced by the glow of the vacuum tubes bleeding through the outer shell of the radio.

"Yes," Jody says aloud. She picks up the remnant of the blunt and takes two more puffs. She slowly turns the small dial at the bottom of the unit. As she does, the large, transparent disk with the frequency numbers printed on it, located above the dial she is turning, starts to rotate.

The sounds coming through the speaker change as she turns the dial. Long moments of static come through in between short burst of silence and then, for a brief moment, she hears a voice. She stops turning the dial but the voice fades.

She turns the dial back very slowly. She hears the same faint voice behind the static and stops. As Jody adjusts the gain control slowly, the noise fades, and the voice becomes more clear.

"F T twenty-eight," she hears through the remaining static. "F T twenty-eight" comes through several seconds later. A sharp bolt of static bursts through the speaker and the voice fades. She spends twenty minutes trying to get it back.

Jody gives up trying for the night and decides, at eleven forty-five, to get some sleep. She shuts the old machine off and goes to bed. Within minutes she is asleep. It doesn't take long for her to start dreaming.

She is strapped to a small chair, looking out of a glass bubble, her hands on the trigger of a machine gun. It takes her a couple of seconds to realize she is in an airplane, ten thousand feet in the air.

"Flight nineteen to Fort Lauderdale tower, do you copy, over," she hears through her headset.

"Lauderdale tower to flight nineteen, go ahead, over."

"We have finished the first leg of our run. We are now adjusting course to three, four, six degrees."

"Confirmed, flight nineteen." There is three minutes of silence.

"Hey, look down there, to the right." The excited voice of a boy barely out of his teens comes through the headset.

"What do you see, Powers?" another young voice asks.

"See those islands down there? That's the Bahamas. That's where I'm retir…"

Jody wakes up quickly, her eyes springing open as her mind continues to process what's just happened. She gets out of bed and heads straight for the cof-fee. She gets ready and heads out to work, her dream lingering in her memory.

Throughout the day her dream continues to occupy her thoughts.

"Are you okay, Jody?" her boss asks. "You've seemed distracted all day." She tells her boss of the strange dream but assures her she will put it out of her mind. It doesn't work.

Jody gets home from work and, for the first time, grabs her laptop. She googles *flight nineteen*. She spends the next couple of hours reading about the ill-fated Navy mission that claimed the lives of twenty-seven men under mysterious conditions.

At eleven o'clock she once again turns the radio on. She adjusts the tuner, trying to find another signal. For nearly half an hour she sits at the radio, and the fresh blunt she lit when she started is half gone.

Through a heavy wave of static she hears a distant voice. Adjusting the gain control, she gets the voice to come in a bit clearer, a bit stronger.

"Both my compasses are out and I'm trying to find Fort Lauderdale, Florida… I am over land but it is broken. I'm sure I'm in the Keys but I…" The signal gets washed away by another blast of strong static. She tries frantically to get the signal back, without any success.

She takes two more puffs then heads off to bed. She closes her eyes and, in what seems to be an instant, she is back in the plane just as the night before. She looks around, trying to remember details.

The sky behind the plane is gray and dismal, light rain occurring sporadically. To her left she sees the aft section of the plane.

"Bombs away," A voice inside her headset says. Three seconds pass.

"Hit," another voice says with excitement. "We got a hit."

Two more planes drop their bombs and the five planes fly off, their mission complete. The group flies for a short time longer.

"Turn to heading three, four, six," Lieutenant Charles Taylor, commander of Flight Nineteen, says over the radio. The squadron complies and the planes turn north in perfect formation.

From the tail gunner position, Jody can see the sky's gray clouds slowly turn to a pale blue. Every cloud's outline vanishes, as does the horizon line of the ocean. The water turns the same color as the clouds. Before long no one knows which way up or down is.

Before anyone can adjust to what is happening, the pale blue atmosphere starts to glow eerily. None of the fourteen other men can see where the glow is coming from but it grows steadily in intensity.

Within minutes the glow is blinding. *These planes look as though they are motionless in a brilliant haze*, Jody thinks to herself, looking out at the formation of planes behind her.

"My compasses are spinning out of control," Lieutenant Taylor says to the rest of his flight. The other four pilots acknowledge the same problem with their planes.

In a matter of seconds, the glowing sky blazes in a blinding flash. When the men regain their senses, the glowing blue sky is returned to its original, rainy gray clouds, thick but now patchy.

Through the openings under them, the pilots see small islands. Taylor doesn't recognize the configuration of land masses.

"Does anyone recognize those islands?" Taylor asks, bewildered.

"This is Lieutenant Stivers," a voice over the radio says. "Those islands look like the Solomons."

"This is Bossi," a different voice comes on. "The Solomon Islands are on the other side of the globe."

"This is Powers," a third voice cuts in. "Stivers is right. The chain we passed looks like the slot. I was there six months ago. I don't know how but Stivers is right."

As the pilots continue to argue about the island chain, the sky becomes the same pale blue they had experienced previously. The glow intensifies rapidly and becomes blinding within seconds.

When her vision returns, Jody sees that the five planes are now flying over frozen tundra.

"What the hell is going on, commander?" she asks in a panic.

"I don't know," Taylor replies, his voice is thick with terror. "Does anyone know what's going on?" All planes report back.

"My fuel tanks are reading empty," Stivers says with panic in his voice.

"Mine are dry as well, skipper," Bossi adds.

"When the first plane goes dry, we'll all ditch together," Taylor tells his men, and within minutes, the first plane radios in the bad news, his engine is out.

"Take them down," Taylor commands. "On the ice." The plane hits the ground hard and, as it skids across the frozen landscape, Jody falls unconscious.

"Jody," a voice screams, followed by a loud, hard pounding on the door. "This is Officer Costello of the Woonsocket Police Department." There is no reply. He pounds on the door several more times.

"Jody, if you don't open the door in ten seconds I'm going to be forced to kick it in." he says but still gets no reply.

"Jody, I'm coming in." Costello says and, on his second try, kicks in the door. He walks into the woman's apartment and cautiously looks around. He passes the kitchen area and heads for the living room. Nothing is out of place.

He enters the living room with the landlord close behind. He sees the short-wave radio on the table. He makes note that the radio is turned on.

Costello makes his way down the small hall at the end of the living room, which leads to the bedroom and bathroom. He enters the bedroom and is taken back by what he sees.

Jody is lying dead on her bed, her face distorted in disbelieving terror. Her skin is bright blue and her lips are purple. She looks as though she is frozen solid.

Costello touches her arm and finds her skin is as hard as a rock and freezing cold. He calls it in and, after a short time, the medical examiner shows up and begins his examination.

He is near completion when two detectives enter the apartment. Costello positions himself to hear their conversation.

"What's the cause of death?" the older of the two asks.

"You're not going to believe it," he replies.

"Try us."

"She's frozen," the M.E. says.

"Frozen?"

"Right to the bone, it looks like. She's solid as a rock."

"Any idea as to the cause?" the younger asks.

"It's only preliminary, mind you," the doctor tells them with a bizarre look on his face. "But to get this frozen she would have to have been in conditions resembling the North Pole… for about seventy-five years."

"But she was at work yesterday," Costello says to himself.

Opportunity Lost

Mike Squatrito

K ona Bali knew this would be an historic day as he climbed into his spacesuit. Minutes later, he arrived from his decompression chamber and approached his landing craft.

A colleague helped adjust his sensory instruments before opening the hatch to the vehicle. "You will make us all proud today." Kona nodded and smiled.

An array of instruments and sensors greeted him as he nestled into his seat. The hatch lowered and sealed with the sound of decompressing air. Kona flipped a switch and the communications link illuminated.

A voice filled the cockpit. "Prepare for biohazard mist." A fine haze enveloped the spacecraft, followed by the sound of gases bonding to the craft's hull.

"Biohazard shield complete."

Kona pressed several buttons, being sure to activate his ship's sensors in the correct operational order.

The voice spoke again. "Preflight checklist complete." A slight pause. "Prepare for engine startup."

Kona swiveled in his mobile cockpit chair and gripped the steering device. The whir of the ion engines filled the area.

"Primary engines engaged."

The eager spaceman looked up to his left and watched a blue light blink three times. After a second delay, the docking bay doors of the mother ship opened, revealing Kona's true objective.

The spaceman's eyes widened, his heart raced faster. Outside the doorway sat the planet that he would investigate. Centuries had passed before his people invented the technology to travel through space, and an even longer time elapsed before they ever found a trace of extraterrestrial existence.

That day finally came. Kona recalled the joy and anxiety he felt when learning of the undeniable proof of alien life. For decades, they followed the steady stream of intelligible radio signals, which led them to this point today.

"Prepare for tractor beam disengagement."

The ion engines whirred faster. Kona scanned the control panel a final time. All was well.

"Tractor beam disengaged." Another slight pause. "Fire engines."

With a rush of adrenaline, Kona blasted the engines forward. The spacecraft propelled out of the docking bay and sped through the emptiness of space at half the speed of light. The small planet grew in size with every passing second as Kona's ship rocketed ever closer.

Kona's people had detected massive amounts of life forms long ago, and he knew that a thriving civilization existed on the surface below. Unbeknownst to these beings, someone had arrived that would change their way of living and thinking forever.

The spaceman maneuvered the vessel at the proper angle to enter the planet's atmosphere. He knew the beings below had the technology to detect him and he had to reach the predefined landing coordinates before that happened. Bringing the spacecraft to the dark side of the planet, the vessel eased through the atmosphere.

A misty covering shrouded Kona's vision, but he guided his ship effortlessly. His eyes rounded after passing through the low level clouds. Massive amounts of an unknown liquid lay below him, stretching for as far as the eye could see.

In the distance, he observed spots of illumination on what appeared to be solid ground. Kona eased forward in his seat, fascinated. Alien creatures are creating those lights! At that moment, he knew that he was the first of his race to view an alien culture with his own eyes. They had sent countless probes to the planet in the past, all with varying levels of success. But to actually *see* an alien city firsthand? Words could not express how he felt.

The vessel steered to the right of the alien metropolis and ventured farther from the unrelenting liquid sea. Large amounts of vegetation appeared below him as the vessel drew closer to the landing site. A moment later, the craft hovered two hundred feet above the planet's surface.

Kona knew he could not communicate with the mother ship in fear of alerting whoever to his presence. His spacecraft was equipped with the best tracking devices, video imaging, and an array of scientific instruments. Kona's commanders would document and analyze his whole trip before officially making first contact.

As the ship began a gentle descent, Kona peered out the windshield, locating an alien residence. Several soft lights glowed from inside a structure. Kona stared in wonderment. How did these creatures live? What was their purpose?

His heart raced faster. A telemetric imaging device guided the ship to the ground. A second later, Kona's spacecraft touched down on the planet — I have landed on an alien world!

Pressing a sequence of buttons placed his ship in a passive mode, which would alert the anxious explorer should anything approach the vessel within a five hundred foot radius. The planet's new visitor grabbed his specimen containers, then prepared himself to leave the craft.

Kona engaged the landing plank, which descended to the planet's surface. A doorway opened and he walked down the strip. Stopping before he reached the strange soil, he gazed downward, knowing he was the first of his race to step onto an alien world. Full of pride, he took that step.

The ground was firm and unlike the land he was accustomed to. Vegetation towered over and around him. Kona opened up his container and began to collect the myriad of flora.

The alien visitor could barely contain himself, but he knew his orders dictated that he spend no more than thirty minutes on the planet's surface. Kona had played out this precise scenario hundreds of times in the simulation laboratories on the mother ship. He knew the vegetation would be useful to study, but he longed for something more alive.

Turning to his right, Kona recalled the alien structure he saw. No, your orders are to gather specimens! He reached for another piece of foliage, placing it in the container. Kona looked over to the right again, seeing the faint illumination a short distance away.

I cannot pass up this opportunity! I must investigate, in the name of science and exploration! Kona hurriedly scampered past his spacecraft and through a thick area of vegetation. A minute later, he found himself on the outskirts of the foreign dwelling. His heart pounded in his chest.

Undeniable proof of intelligent alien existence! His sensors alerted him that there was something definitely alive and moving inside. Kona thought for a moment, wondering if he should just go back to his assigned task, but his mind yearned for more.

Against his better judgment, he darted toward the dwelling. Several buildings made up the complex, with one of them having a large, open doorway. His sensors flashed repeatedly, signaling the abundance of life forms.

Kona carefully approached the opening, using his instruments to guide him in the waning light. Outlines of creatures appeared everywhere. His heart pounded, seemingly ready to burst from his chest. Kona's environmental sensors adjusted his airflow to accommodate his shallow breathing and his body returned to a relatively normal state of excitement.

To the left of the structure sat a mechanical vehicle. The spaceman scanned the object, fascinated at what these creatures might have used it for. With his imaging scan completed, he began to focus on the next structure. An internal cue reminded him that he had less than ten minutes before the completion of his mission.

Kona had just begun to make his next move when a sensor alerted him of movements from behind. The alien visitor turned to see a bright flash, then a searing pain filled his chest cavity. Horrified, he dropped to the unfamiliar ground, his bodysuit sending him an overload of information.

"Catastrophic system failure. Mission Aborted!"

The phrase rang inside Kona's head and he knew what that meant. A final indicator informed him that his internal systems were compiling an event log of his mission and that his external suit would cease to work in five seconds. Without his bodysuit, he would become vulnerable to the planet's harsh environment. Furthermore, no one would come looking for him.

A final transmission on a preprogrammed frequency alerted the mother ship in a little more than a nanosecond that the mission failed. Then, system abort. Kona's life force waned the moment his bodysuit turned off. Pain overtook his body, his damaged heart beat irregularly, and his breathing became erratic.

Before death relieved him of his anguish, Kona saw two creatures approach him. One hunched over and seemed to look into his eyes. Then, all went dark.

The creature stood back up. "Jesus, Jeb, I think it's a goddam Martian!"

The second person lowered his rifle. "I told ya I saw somethin' in the sky! I'm gonna call the sheriff! Get away from that thing!"

A Night's Tale

A.Keith Carreiro

This is only one of many stories of Lucien d'Athanase. Twelve glories he garnered before he was knighted, before he became the argent weapon of a high king's right arm. He was at that time in life when one leaves childhood and begins to grow into the fullness of the man or woman they become. There was neither king nor kingdom then.

Powerful lords ruled over the land. Each was a virtual king. Not only was the might of their weapons used to carve out such realms. The coin they collected in their individual demesnes was visible evidence and assertion of their authority to make such demands. They waged war with it just as much as they did with their armed men and trebuchets.

Their minds never sought peace, but power, instead.

Lucien had worked all day in the field with his father. As dusk settled around them, they quit their work and returned home for their evening meal. Once in their croft and with no intention of being unkind, Lucien fell asleep in a chair in front of the fire. His parents, out of compassion for the work he had done for that day, and for the many days stretching out in the past—as well as what lay before them in the growing season—left him to his rest.

In his dream he felt the raw cold of winter erupt against his awareness. Dirt and dust from the road he was on blew by him in sustained waves of red. It felt as if he were standing in the middle of a river whose surface rapidly streamed away from him. Or, as if he stood just at the inside edge of a beach, the water surging through his legs back into the ocean while his feet adjusted to the shifting sand underneath him.

Despite the raw cold, his woolen clothes, long coat, scarf and boots helped stave off the freezing air.

For a while, perhaps eleven or twelve seemingly slow heartbeats, he could not see where he was. He thought he heard a series of low moans, but could not be sure if it was the wind making such a noise or something living that was in great distress.

The wind ceased.

The dust settled.

The cold air weighted him in place.

The land that stretched around him into the far distance was unfamiliar. A town lay about a half a mile before him.

On both sides of the road, and as far as he could see in back of him and before him, people hung on crosses. Many were dead. The few who were not, remained senseless.

Five hundred feet ahead of him, three young men stood in front of one of the crosses. They were shouting at one another.

Lucien could only hear the sound of their voices and not what they were saying.

While he walked toward them, he took the time to look more closely at his surroundings.

His boots made a slight scrunching sound on the road.

Broken-down carts and the scattered belongings of many people fleeing away from the town littered both sides of the road. A child's doll lay on its back in a distorted position. One of its legs was torn in half. The face was scuffed beyond recognition.

For some reason this disfigured toy caused him more distress than anything else that he was observing.

The wind shifted 180 degrees and was now beating against him. He smelled something burning and could see that part of the town was on fire.

He had cut the distance to the young men in half, and could now hear some of their shouted words to one another.

There were no clouds in the sky. Even so, the winter sunlight lacked any strength of heat.

I wonder why there are no birds.

He looked around for them. But he could neither see nor hear any sign of them.

When he was a hundred feet away from the men they stopped their argument with one another. The three turned around from facing the broken man on the cross and stared petulantly at Lucien. They remained silent until he stood directly before them.

"What have we here," the tallest one said.

He was fair-haired and dressed as a young nobleman. He wore a long dark fur coat that opened as he waved his arms in argument with the other two men. He had a sword strapped to his waist that hung from a leather belt on his left side.

Sweat poured down his face. His hat and shirt were stained from it.

"So now we have another miscreant wandering in our midst."

Lucien said nothing.

"Looks innocent enough," stated the man with light brown hair. He was wearing grey clothing. A crossbow hung on his back. "What's your name?"

"Lucien."

"Lucien what?" asked the third man.

"d'Athanase."

"Hummph," snorted the tall man. "What kind of man dressed like a peasant carries such a landed surname?"

"Ignore him, Lucien," said the second man. "Hafrin may look like a peacock in a bear's skin, but he mostly struts and clucks a lot. My name's Elaeth. This one here," referring to the man wearing a dark green cloak, "is Owaine."

Lucien nodded at them.

The men turned back to look once more at the man on the cross.

"Look, this one here needs to be taken down, like I said. The sooner the better."

"And we keep tellin' you, Hafrin," Elaeth stated, "that we need to get off this bloody cold road and into the town."

"Yeah, the sooner the better," Owaine said.

"This fellow doesn't belong here!" Hafrin shouted. "I don't care about the bloody cold or the town."

Elaeth saw that Lucien was looking at the three of them with a puzzled look. "Aye," he affirmed, "this lot," indicating Hafrin, "is bollocksed beyond repair."

Lucien looked askance at the man on the cross. Most of the remaining clothes on him were in tatters. He had been severely beaten. His chest, stomach, and thighs were scarred from the punishment meted out to him. Like the child's doll Lucien saw abandoned on the road, the man's face was completely unrecognizable.

Elaeth addressed Hafrin again. "See how the young lad . . . Lucien, is it?"

Lucien nodded.

". . . is at a loss to wonder what you're goin' on about, Hafrin."

"I told you over and over again, this fellow needs to be taken down off the cross."

"You're not makin' any sense," said Owaine, "as usual. You've got this refrain in your head that makes you sound idiotic."

"I don't care what you have to say. We're takin' him off the beam."

"C'mon, Owaine," said Elaeth, "let's just go into the town and leave this madness alone. Hafrin can take him down by himself—unless Lucien wants to help him."

Lucien shook his head, indicating he wanted nothing to do with it. He looked toward the gates of the town and saw that the crosses began there. They were staggered about twenty-five feet apart from and opposite one another.

It had to have taken a large number of soldiers to do such a grisly task, he thought.

He gazed at their placed procession on both sides of the road as they stretched by him and receded into the distance away from the town.

Without saying anything, Lucien started walking. He kept his eyes straight ahead of him and tried to focus just on the front gates of the town.

Striding away from the young men, he heard their argument break out afresh. Insults were thrown back and forth.

Soon enough, their ridicule and scorn against each other almost faded away completely.

Approaching the gate, he stepped into the shadow of the town's outer wall. The iron-plated portcullis was raised. Its spiked ends gleamed dully above him in the shaded light. Both of the sides of the arched gate were each about fifteen feet wide. They were made of oak and studded with iron bolts that formed a series of concentric patterns emanating around the wicket or pedestrian gate inset within each side of the larger one.

He announced himself aloud to indicate he wanted to pass through the entryway into the town.

No one responded, even after several attempts to gain notice.

He tried each of the smaller doors. They were locked.

He could not even budge the larger gates.

He heard footsteps in back of him.

"What, no one home?"

He turned around and saw that Elaeth was by himself.

Elaeth turned back toward the road and pointed to his two disparate companions, one trailing the other in the distance.

"Yes, they're still arguing with one another. You'd swear they were married."

He turned back to the gateway. "Wicket doors bolted?"

"Yes," responded Lucien.

"Can't move either of the big doors?"

Lucien shook his head.

Elaeth went over and examined the big doors. He tried, first, to push them open. Nothing moved. Next, he tried pulling on them. The result of his second effort was equally fruitless.

"Let's wait for the other two to get here and then see if the four of us can get it open."

Lucien leaned against the left side of the wicket door. He drifted away in thought and then was startled by feeling the door tremble. Just as he was going to say something about it, Owaine walked into the shadow of the town entranceway.

"Well, that's quite proper to wait for me before goin' in."

Not directly responding to Owaine, Elaeth explained that the doors were not opening and that perhaps the four of them could see if they could work one of the bigger doors aside enough to squeeze through the gate.

Soon enough, Hafrin arrived. He was completely out of sorts. Putting his hands on his hips, he said, "What, now you're polite and waiting for me to be with you before we proceed into the town?"

Both of his companions failed to answer. They just stared at Hafrin.

"What's the matter with you two?"

Still no response.

Hafrin looked at Lucien. "And . . ."

"We need the four of us to maneuver either of the big doors open."

"Did you try the wicket doors?" Hafrin asked.

"Yes!" came back the response from the three before him.

"Well, is it bolted from the inside?"

"Yes!"

"Did you try them, or are you just guessing?"

Exasperated, Owaine berated him. "Just help us see if we can get the big doors to move a bit."

"Then what?" Hafrin asked.

"We go into the town," Owaine said.

"Why don't you pick the lock?"

"Hafrin, these doors don't have locks, they're both bolted."

"Come on, take the crown off your head and help us," urged Elaeth.

Elaeth went to the left side of the gateway and urged all four of them to put their shoulders to the gate and push at the same time.

Nothing happened.

They tried again three more times.

Failing to push the left side of the door even a finger-width open, they turned their attention and efforts to the right side.

With the same result. Nothing.

Another argument flared up.

Disgusted, Lucien went over to the left wicket gate and sat on the ground with his back against it.

The three original companions argued on about doors, entrance ways, castle gates, murder holes, fortifications, traps for the unwary, and the lack of sense everyone else had.

As this dispute unfolded, Lucien again felt the door against which he sat shake. This happened several more times, with each successive vibration increasing in its force.

With the altercation of opinions now at its fever pitch before him, he thought he heard a metal hinge bolt drop to the ground and reverberate on stone pavement. The wooden bolt holding the door clattered after it.

He stood up, faced the doorway, and pushed.

The door swung all the way open.

He stepped through, and went almost all the way to the end of the arched entryway. He stopped and looked back at the young men who were now staring silently at him.

While they stayed in place, he went back to where they stood.

"Well?" he asked.

All three rushed the door at once, as if it would slam shut on them before they could use it.

Running through the full width of the enclosed gateway, they now stood in the place that Lucien had first reached. They looked back at him.

As Lucien went to close the wicket door, he looked out at the road he had just traveled on. All the crosses with the people on them were gone. In their place were fully grown, incense cedar trees.

By the time they had walked the deserted streets to the castle itself, which stood at the top of a steep hill in the center of the town, the sun was about to set.

Dusk was approaching.

The cold intensified, looming ever deeper into a raw weight of gelid thickness.

The fire he had first seen burning in the town seem to be limited still to the same area. On his way over to the castle the fire remained where he had first noted it. Only a slight taint of scorched wood and wisp of smoke from what fed its hunger teased his sense of smell.

Another gateway faced them.

This one was far smaller than the one in which they gained entrance into the town. The large wooden door was open. Made of two layers of oak planks, the seasoned grain of the wood ran up and down on its front side, while running horizontally across on its inside. Held together by iron studs, it was strengthened and reinforced with darkly stained iron bands.

They passed through two sets of crenellated walls and a killing field.

As the gloom of dusk thickened, they reached a paved walkway in the courtyard that led into the castle interior. Its crystalline, herringbone pattern was filled with mica. The remaining captured light that was still caught in its design lit up their way.

They passed a well where they stopped, and as Lucien walked up a marble stairway leading to the first floor, the other three young men argued whether or not to drink the water from the well.

"I'm bloody thirsty," Owaine half lamented and complained.

"For all you know, it's poisoned," Hafrin stated.

Back and forth followed retort after retort.

When it got to the point where minds blurred and blows started, Lucien walked back to Elaeth's side and urged them to go into the castle's kitchen, pantry, or the buttery itself.

"I'm sure there will be plenty of food and drink to be had at your pleasure," he informed them.

Hafrin tried to argue about the sense of such counsel.

The other two told him to hold his tongue.

Lucien guided them up the southern stairway onto the first floor of the castle.

They reached a corbeled arched corridor that ran out of sight into the recesses of the first floor. Their footsteps rang onto a burnished flagstone floor. Light with an unknown source radiated throughout the interior.

Lucien thought its brightness was playing tricks on what he was seeing. It was as though a mist arose from the floor. Like a fog, the brume slowly swirled in place and seemed to shift around in the distance so that it did not simply remain in place in one spot. It was a subtle shift of perception and not something that he could say was clearly permanent to his line of sight.

Behind them stood a small armory.

Luxuriously woven rugs were displayed on the walls. Their patterns were in earth colors and contained a variety of hunting scenes. The walls were plastered in an off-ivory white and pebbled pattern.

They hugged the right side of the vast corridor.

The first room they passed was the garrison quarters for the castle defenders.

An empty mess hall was next. Only long wooden tables and their benches were in place.

The officers' hall followed. It was on their left.

They entered a smaller corridor where a pantry was on one side and a kitchen was on the other.

There was no evidence of anyone alive.

Ahead was the guard room, and to its right, a round arched doorway led into a great hall.

The redolent odor of a feast just prepared and set wafted from its interior toward them.

Their mouths watered. They could think of nothing now but food and drink.

As they entered the hall, three massive candelabra hung from the ceiling and poured out a golden glow that made everything seem unique, treasured and precious.

Long tables set with white linens were in the middle of the hall.

On a center table stood an array of food, still fresh and hot. Reddish-purple carrots, onions, and beets glistened in their bowls, thick slices of brown bread used as trenchers to soak up juice and sauce from the food, and suckling pig seasoned with cinnamon, ginger, nutmeg, and bitter orange peel, were all set upon the table.

Ale, beer, red and white wines, mead, and cider were arrayed throughout each table with plenty of cups, goblets, and flagons from which to drink.

Hafrin, his pale blue eyes in a shock of hunger and greed, wiped the saliva dripping from his lips.

Elaeth took the crossbow from his back and leaned it unconsciously against the nearest table where he was standing, in awe of the repast before him.

Owaine went to the drink first. He removed his dark green cloak and draped it over the edge of a table.

In a daze, he exclaimed, "How do we know this seductive magic before us is not as poisonous as the well water we passed below in the court-yard?"

"Now that I see what is before me, I cannot recall when I last ate," wondered Elaeth.

The light in the great hall seemed to become even more golden, making everything resplendent and singular in its own right.

Hafrin, acting half-asleep yet half-awake, uttered, "I cannot recall ever seeing such a banquet."

He walked over to the food and served himself everything he could load on the trencher he had in his hands.

The other two joined him at the same table where he had seated himself. For once, no dispute was enjoined among them.

The light in the room sparkled once more.

For some reason, Lucien thought of the wicket door again as it shook slightly against him. He almost expected the brightness to fall to the stone floor and give off echoes of color instead of the sound of metal clanging against it.

The sight of the men gorging themselves at table turned him away from them.

He walked out of the great room and back into the corridor. He retraced his steps to the southern side of the castle stairs. He went up the stairs to the third floor.

The corridor here was empaneled with a variety of light- and dark-toned woods. Oak, flame maple, pine, spruce, and even Claro walnut adorned the floor and walls. Massive pine beams with pitch-pine, cross-beams topped with teak boards, were in the ceiling above him.

Again staying to the right side of the vaulted corridor, he went by another garrison room and great hall positioned on the second floor as well. Both rooms were fully furnished.

No one was present.

The silence became an uproar.

At the north end of the castle, he espied an open door. Light flickered inside it.

Entering fully into the room, he discovered he was in a large solar. The floor was made of burl maple wood planks, polished to a saffron luster. Three thick, large wool rugs were arrayed next to one another. They displayed abstract patterns in a wide variety of soft colors.

Chairs and couches were amply placed throughout the great chamber. Made of damask, the reversible figured fabrics of cotton, wool, linen, and silk contained a variety of woven polychromed and single-color images. Mythical beasts pounced and hunted on their satin and sateen woven scenes.

A large and lit crystal candelabrum hung in the middle of the room. The ceiling above was painted in a profoundly blue, star-like decoration. Looking at it in deep admiration for the skill in which it was made, Lucien felt as though he was floating into the sky.

He looked away from it quickly.

Bas-relief columns, eight on each side of the room, ran two-thirds of the length of the walls with the top of them splaying out in a half-circle containing twelve fluted edges.

A fire burned with great force in a hearth built into the central part of the far wall. A triptych of marble was inset as a mantel above and around its sides. Two griffins were pictured opposite a newly arisen phoenix, while an elongated dragon swallowing its tail wrapped itself around the whole image.

The fire sizzled and crackled with a gusto that became a mystery to him. There was nothing there to make it burn. Flames wove, bent, and scintillated on an invisible fuel.

Three great tapestries adorned the walls. Just as he was about to examine the one to the left side of the fireplace, a figure detached itself from the wall.

Startled sufficiently into a state of shock, Lucien gasped and dropped to his knees. His eyes looked at the deep crimson color of the rug underneath him.

A pleasant voice, baritone in pitch, resounded throughout the room.

"Ah, you must excuse me, Lucien. I forget that I sometimes startle people when they see me for the first time."

Lucien kept looking at the carpet. The color of the rug started to change to a deep scarlet hue. He swayed in place.

"Here, here, young man," said the voice, "we can't have you like this. Please, stand up and come sit down near the fire."

Lucien felt powerful yet gentle hands help him to stand. He was led carefully over to the hearth and guided safely to sit on a large chair.

The fire snapped as if in applause to his ability, even with assistance, to stand, walk, and sit in a chair.

He looked up at the man. He saw someone who was about five feet ten inches tall. His hair was silver and long, and accompanied a strong square face, grey eyes and a full beard. He was dressed in the guise of a hermit.

The man looked at him directly.

"There, that's better. My name is Myrddin, And yours is Lucien d'Athenase."

Lucien tried to find his voice. Not a sound came out of him except for the loud beating of his heart pounding in agitation in his head.

Myrddin excused himself, went into an adjoining room. He brought back with him a glass decanter of fresh spring water and a cup. He filled the cup half full and handed it to Lucien.

Lucien took it with his right hand, but failed to raise it to his lips.

"Drink," Myrddin urged him.

Seeing that a drink was in his hand, he brought it to his mouth. After an initial swallow, he drank again and emptied the cup.

"Thank you, Myrddin," Lucien said.

"Well, that's better. Good to hear your voice, lad."

Looking around in wonder, Lucien asked, "Where am I?"

"Why, you're in the manor of a great war lord, son."

Lucien shook his head in confusion.

"Your three companions, all children of wrath, with whom you entered the town and this castle, have completely gorged themselves. They are asleep at table from their dinner exertions." Myrddin smiled, more to himself than to Lucien.

Lucien looked around the room as if seeing it for the first time.

"This is a wondrous place, Myrddin."

"Indeed."

"Have I died?"

"Not at all, not at all. You're just visiting."

For some reason, the old man's remark did not disturb him.

Lucien looked again at the tapestries on the walls.

He stood up and walked over to the one that was to the left of the hearth.

Three women were pictured standing at the back of a table inside an opened atrium built in fieldstone that looked out upon a lake. Before them was set a large chalice. Flames were depicted on the ceiling above them. Outside the door of the atrium a young man dressed in a satin and silk robe was kneeling before them. His hands were clasped. Three angels stood together in a row in back of the young man. They were attired in light golden robes.

Lucien could not tell whether or not the angels held javelins or staffs in their hands. In the left hand of the angel closest to the kneeling man was a scroll extended out in his direction.

On the edge of the water were two knights. One, an older man, was kneeling; the other, a younger man, was standing. They each held the same kind of weapon or staff as the angels. Their shields were on their left.

"This is a wondrous vision."

"Quite so," replied Myrddin. "It's called *True Love*."

Lucien stared at the tapestry.

After a while, Myrddin asked the young man if he would like to look at the second tapestry of his own choosing.

"Please," Lucien said.

He looked at the tapestry hanging on the opposite wall and walked over to it. The scene shown was cast in blues. Two armies were locked in gruesome and pitched combat against each other. The plain on which they fought looked exactly like the one where he had just been. He realized the town and castle woven into the image were the same as the ones where he was now standing.

His eyes opened wide.

"It's called the *Trail of Light*," Myrddin said.

Lucien walked back to the hearth and examined the tapestry to the right of the hearth.

The fire stayed bright and burned with a sound like a deeply struck harp string.

The third tapestry was set on its end rather than affixed in a landscape position. Five borders were around the outside edge, four narrow and one wide. The outside edge had a beaded pattern wherein blue, gold, and tan colors followed one another in random order. It was centered between two borders of gold. A wide band of flowers containing hibiscus, snapdragons, peonies, and other flowers Lucien could not identify were enfolded amongst branches and leaves. A thin border of looped rope followed. The major scene in the middle of the tapestry depicted a tree resembling an ancient copper beech. The side of its trunk shone in a soft silver against a black background. The deep burgundy-purple color of its leaves shimmered, making everything appear as if it were cast in crimson and amaranth.

"This is the *Tree of Life*," Myrddin said softly.

Lucien sighed deeply. He walked back to his chair and sat down. He remained deep in thought.

"Which one would you like to take with you, Lucien?"

The young man looked at the hermit with deep confusion.

"Which tapestry would you like me to give you?" Myrddin repeated. "For yourself," he added.

"It is with deep honor unto itself to just look upon them once in a lifetime."

"True, boy. But humor me: if you took one, which one would you like."

"Myrddin, this place is no ordinary one. To take something as precious as these would not be a rightful choice. I would feel that I had done a great wrong no matter the beauty each one holds. Instead of my taking one, can I not take the offer of one to me as a gift in which we, in turn, give back to the land so that peace may arise?"

Myrddin smiled at the young man.

He looked at the fire burning away in the hearth and said, "You may begin."

Three streams of light poured out of the fire and each one raced to its respective tapestry.

The scenes from all three tapestries detached themselves from their woven backings as each swirled finger of fire touched them. Rolled up into these singular coils of scintillant flame, they shimmered like the northern lights, but these were gleaming in just one large room, instead of their undulating under an open sky.

Looking at the light bending in and out through the solar, Myrddin extended his right hand toward the decanter he had brought into the room earlier. The radiance that had spread out now gathered itself together and poured itself into the glass bottle. It flared brightly for a brief moment then became still. Bubbles of light raced to the top of the decanter.

The old man walked over to the carafe and placed its liquid radiance into the young man's cup. Myrddin, holding the cup in his hands, handed it to Lucien.

"Drink," he offered.

Lucien did not remember taking it.

He only remembered the last swallow he took.

He awoke with a start. He was in the chair he had fallen asleep in at his home.

The fire flared and burned brightly.

Lucien saw something gleaming on the floor to the right side of the fire.

He went over to it and picked it up, looking at it closely in wonder.

Gathered around a cup of silver was the shimmering image of three coiled lines of fire.

Class Day

Sam Kafrissen

Jack had been looking forward to Class Day for weeks. It would be the last time his ninth grade class at Hugh B. Bain Junior High would be together as a group. Several of his good friends would be going to the new high school, to be called *West*, on the other side of town next year. Jack and the others would be going to the old school that hereafter would be called *East*. Planning for Class Day had been in the works for months with the final decision being that the group would celebrate their graduation from junior high at Rocky Point, one of the largest and most popular amusement parks in New England. It had the fastest and steepest roller coaster, the tallest Ferris wheel, the treacherous Wild Mouse, and an enormous shore dinner hall famous for its clam cakes and chowder.

Just a few weeks before Class Day, Jack had started seeing a new girl named Kathy Souza. Kathy was Portuguese and had dark hair and dark brown eyes with an amazingly piercing look. It was only later in their time together that Jack learned she was wearing contact lenses, a relatively new product few families he knew could afford. Jack and Kathy had flirted with each other in homeroom for a couple of years, but it seemed that one or the other was always going steady with someone else. Unlike Kathy, who was a serious student, Jack's grades were generally pretty mediocre. Yet he had always loved school because of the girls. He'd discovered them as early as first grade and life was never the same afterwards. Having grown up in a household full of boys, Jack found girls to be a mysterious but intriguing breed apart. Once he started hugging and kissing them there was no end to the joys they brought to his young life.

Jack still liked doing the usual boyish things with his guy friends: playing sports, sneaking cigarettes, and wising off in school. But he could never understand those boys who said they *hated* girls. For Jack, girls were soft and cuddly and well, they were just different from boys. He loved their barely formed adolescent bodies, their long hair, and most of all their sweet smell. Even when they sweated, girls never seemed to smell skunky like guys did.

In the summer, Jack would spend hours at the beach staring at teenage girls with their long bare legs and protruding breasts. Unlike some of the faster girls, Kathy Souza was still pretty unschooled in the adolescent art of petting – which consisted primarily of holding hands, hugging, and kissing until your lips hurt. When Jack first tried to tongue Kathy, she told him he was a *pervert*. She blocked each of his forays with her gleaming white teeth. Jack retreated for a few days, then mounted another assault, this time in a gentler fashion. Eventually Kathy relented and even came to enjoy his probing. Of late she'd begun to experiment in kind.

With Class Day fast approaching, Jack was looking forward to deep kissing Kathy at the top of the Rocky Point Ferris wheel. He envisioned them sitting alone in their car on top of the world, just the two of them – young and in love. The student council had raised enough money to hire two motor coaches for the long trip down the bay to Rocky Point. Man, this was luxury, Jack thought. For once they would not be riding in rickety old school buses that often broke down. That would have been a disaster on Class Day.

Jack and Kathy sat in the back of the Greyhound Motor Coach away from the chaperones, where they could hold hands and even kiss furtively on the way to the park. That day Kathy wore white shorts, which contrasted nicely with her naturally bronzed legs. Jack was feeling particularly like a stud in his T-shirt and dungarees, clothes the boys were prohibited from wearing during regular school days.

When they arrived at the park, the students were issued prepaid passes that would allow them to enjoy as many rides as they wished. They would, however, have to use their own money for food and any games of chance they played down along the midway. Jack quickly dropped a dollar playing skee-ball, shooting pop rifles at the laughing clowns, and tossing baseballs at milk bottles, all in a failed effort to win a large stuffed animal for his new girlfriend. The day was going just swell, though Jack did not like the helplessness he felt when the carny men on the midway made suggestive comments or ogled Kathy and some of the other girls with their menacing eyes.

Jack and Kathy rode the roller coaster twice. Although he was a bit frightened of it, Jack didn't let on. When it rushed downward, he simply closed his eyes and screamed like all the other kids, even though he was screaming from fear rather than thrill. They tried three times to get onto the Ferris wheel, but the lines were always too long. Kathy shrugged and said they could try again after lunch. As noon neared, the shore dinner hall began to fill up. Still, the place was enormous, so they had no problem finding a seat at a picnic table with some of the other kids. They each ordered a half-dozen clam cakes, a cup of chowder, Cokes, and watermelon for dessert. Jack offered to pay for Kathy, but thankfully she insisted upon paying for herself. If she had accepted, Jack would've been tapped out. Besides, he still hoped to get another shot at winning her a stuffed animal before the day was over.

Kathy ate only three of her clam cakes and half of her chowder, so Jack finished them off along with his own. As a result, by the time they left the shore dinner hall, Jack was feeling a little bloated. They tried the Ferris wheel again but the line was still too long. At Kathy's insistence they rode on the Spinning Teacups, which in Jack's eyes wasn't much of a ride. It was designed mostly for little kids. He went along anyway to please Kathy and get another chance to lay his arm across her shoulder and pull her in close. The two of them were getting along so well, Jack was determined that if they ever got to the top of the Ferris wheel he'd ask Kathy to go steady with him, maybe even give her the black onyx ring he'd gotten from his Aunt Harriet last Christmas.

The only big ride they hadn't been on yet was the Wild Mouse, a smaller but no less harrowing version of a roller coaster. For this ride, two riders would be bolted into a car side by side. The Mouse would then motor around a track at ever increasing speeds. What made the ride so exciting and frightening was that the cars were much wider than the track so at every corner, riders had the sensation that they would fly right off into space. This particular Wild Mouse also tilted inward as it picked up speed. Jack and Kathy were put in the front seat so they could experience the full impact of each abrupt turn. The Wild Mouse was notorious for leaving its riders very dizzy. Passersby often had a good laugh watching riders exit the Mouse, stumbling and reeling before they regained their sense of balance. Some passengers even fell to the ground as they tottered down the exit ramp. Jack was not a big fan of the Wild Mouse, but when Kathy dragged him into the line there was no turning back.

At first, Jack simply smiled at Kathy when their car started to careen slowly down the track. Before long, the full force of the ride began to take hold of Jack - along with the nine clam cakes, two cups of chowder, Coke, and watermelon in his stomach. As the cars dashed into each hair-raising turn, Jack could feel the food rising up into his throat. Then without warning, his entire lunch came up and was spewed across Kathy's bright white shorts and down her deeply tanned legs. Kathy screamed but her screams were drowned out by those of the other passengers on the ride.

It wasn't until the Wild Mouse came to a complete stop that Jack and everyone else could survey the full damage of what he'd done. Kathy was mortified. She was literally covered from waist to foot in Jack's vomit. As soon as the restraining bar was raised, she leaped from their car and sped in the direction of the women's restroom. There she was joined by two of her girlfriends who had noticed her condition. Jack staggered to the nearest bench, holding his stomach in agony. Although he felt awful, he was glad to be rid of the shore dinner. He had dribbled some vomit down his own shirtfront, but it was Kathy who'd been on the receiving end of most of his discharge.

Jack waited for what seemed like the longest time for her to emerge from the girls' room. When she did, she was brusquely ushered by her girl-friends in a direction away from where Jack was sitting. Despite wanting to chase after her, he still felt too awful to move. Finally he just lay down on the bench and closed his eyes, praying that the nausea would pass. He must have fallen asleep, because the next thing he knew he was being jabbed by Tommy Jarrell, who told him the buses were loading for the trip back home. By the time Jack stumbled to the lot, one bus was already filled and the other had only a few seats left, all in the front where the chaperones and uncool kids sat. Jack looked for Kathy but she was nowhere to be seen; she must've gotten on the other bus. He still felt ill, so he took whatever seat was left and slept all the way back.

He awoke just as his bus pulled up in front of the school. He wanted to get off quickly so he could at least tell Kathy how sorry he was for throw-ing up on her. Unfortunately, the other bus had already discharged its pas-sengers. Through the window he could see Kathy ducking into Linda Ferensi's mother's car. She had a green sweater tied around her waist, no doubt to cover up the stains on her white shorts.

Once at home, Jack fell into bed, after mumbling to his mother about how he'd gotten sick at the park. She came in once and tried to ask him about the trip but Jack was in no mood to talk. She felt his forehead for a fever and then pulled the covers up over him. By morning he had recovered enough to feel recriminations about what had happened at Rocky Point. He tried calling Kathy all that day without getting an answer. The same was true the next day as well.

On the third day, Jack decided to ride his bike over to Kathy's house, which was no mean feat given that she lived up near the dairy farms on the far side of town. It was a good five-mile ride made longer by the hot June sun. Jack was worn out by the time he got there. It took him a while to screw up the courage to ring her doorbell. He'd never been to Kathy's before and was surprised at how lavish her house was compared to his more modest home.

When he pushed the button, the bell made a chiming sound that echoed throughout the house. Jack waited but heard no other sounds from within. He put his face up against the glass, though he couldn't detect any movement inside. He pushed the bell again, this time holding it for a few seconds. Still nothing. As Jack turned to leave, the door swung open and an older, attractive version of Kathy stood in the doorway. The woman's dark hair was frosted with blond streaks and she wore a lot of what looked like expensive jewelry.

"Can I help you, young man?" she asked with just a hint of disdain in her voice.

"Yea, um," Jack stammered. "I was uh, wondering if Kathy was home."

The woman shook her head. "No, Kathy's off to camp. Her father and I dropped her there over the weekend. She won't be home again until the end of August. Who should I tell her came calling?"

Jack hesitated for a moment. "It's not important. I'm just a friend from school. I was out riding my bike and I just thought I'd…" Jack never finished what he wanted to say.

Mrs. Souza looked past Jack around the open fields where no one just casually rode his bike. "Well. Fine. It was pleasant meeting you," she said without meaning it. "I hope you have a nice summer." Kathy's mother then abruptly shut the door in Jack's face.

It was a much longer ride home as Jack dawdled along the way, thinking about Kathy and how they never did get to ride the Ferris wheel and how he never did ask her to go steady with him. He also felt bad about not asking Kathy's mother for her address at camp so he could at least write her an apology. Jack never saw Kathy Souza again. In the fall he went to East and Kathy to West. Within the first week of high school Jack had a new girlfriend. Her name was Susan.

Final Harvest

Jack Nolan

Will couldn't sleep, a full ten months after Jenny died, and it had him worn to a nub and angry over it. He stumbled through the final harvest like a blind man, twice slumping over in the cab of the Massey Ferguson combine, carving highways through the heart of the straw before coming to, like to kill somebody. Day-hands told him they'd quit if it kept up, but Will got through it, delivered the crop, paid 'em off, sent 'em packing. The auctioneer told him bidding would go higher if he was there, so he made himself sit on the porch with the numbers droning in his head like a beehive, rocking to keep awake, watching strangers and some lifetime neighbors buy off everything, from the rusty Allis-Chalmers tractor father had taught him to drive when he was 12, right down to the black fire-place tools Jenny gave him on a Christmas morning long ago. It was all bad enough already, but having to go through it without one decent night's sleep, it just seemed little enough to ask The Good Lord for.

It was no better now, with most everything settled. Ruth and Rizzy were gone, having hugged him and driven off right after he closed on the little house in town they said would be just perfect for him. Movers coming here day after next to haul boxes of personal gear into what the daughters called his "new life." And after forty years of fighting to break even, the sale of the farm put more in the bank than he'd ever hoped to see. So with everything settled, why couldn't a long, hard day end with his prayer-talk with Jenny and The Good Lord, a familiar passage from Scripture, and then deep, sound sleep, like always before?

Determined to be rid of it tonight, he had his bourbon, more than Jenny allowed, starting out neat for the one he cradled in front of the TV news, watering down the ones he sipped while making dinner, eating, doing up the dishes. Then he pulled on his PJs and lay in bed reading his Bible for half an hour, but still wasn't sleepy when he shut off the light. He wasn't supposed to take the pills Doc gave him with alcohol, so he skipped them. They did no good either way, with or without bourbon. Sleeping in the guest room downstairs was no use, neither was staying up even later or drinking lots or nothing, eating more or eating less, along with everything else, none of it made any gull-durned difference anyhow. Even sleeping wore him out, seemed. Will rolled onto his side and tried to think simple thoughts, to drive away earthly cares and leave for tomorrow what must be done tomorrow, and sometime around midnight, he slept.

Anger's a sin. But when thunder rattled the house, shaking him awake just after two o'clock, he pulled himself to the bathroom madder than all get out. He muttered while he took a leak, washed up and stumbled back toward bed, using modest cuss words that were the only profanities he permitted. Men that Will grew up around didn't ever admit out loud to feeling tired, and it wasn't his nature to complain. But in his life, all the solitary days way out in the open fields or around animals, through the hard toil of working the farm, he never felt this dog-tired. It was like the fields and the animals needed him, depended on his strength, and now with the livestock shipped off and the land passing to someone else, his vitality just poured out into an empty hole.

Will thought this must be what it's like when someone loses his mind. Middle of the night, lightning flashing through the curtains into the big hollow house, empty of most its furniture, thunder shaking it to the foundation, Will figured this had to be close enough to what craziness must be like — muttering to yourself in the dark and filled up with an anger that never went away.

White flashes lit the walls built by his father and grandfather, wife and mother and grandmother, three generations had prayed and laughed here, the Hofstetter Farm. This was the only world Will had ever known or needed for all his sixty-two years. School buses had pulled up by the big mailbox out front for him and then for his sisters and when the last of them had married and moved away, the buses came for his and Jenny's daughters, Ruth and Rizzy, in just about an endless stream, every year from 1940, when he started first grade, until Rizzy had gone away to college in 1992. Yellow buses honking at the mailbox for most of fifty-two years. But for a long stretch of time, he and Jenny knew this wasn't permanent, this farm and the life on it, like Will's father had thought it would be. Farming changed, generations changed, and from the time Rizzy was nine, Will and Jenny had looked across the dinner table at their daughters and had known there was going to be nobody to carry it on. Those young minds were settling on other things than being a wife on a corn and soybean operation, some hay and cattle and a few chickens to give the kids something to do.

During the week after Jenny went up to heaven, the idea seemed to take the girls by surprise, somehow, that this would be the end of it. It hadn't seemed to dawn on them until then, this sad knowledge that Will had chewed on and swallowed with every dinner they shared together for two decades. They had been happy children, pulling top honors in school, prizes in music and athletics, proud of themselves and sure that they were bringing joy to their parents. They missed Jenny's hand reaching out for Will's, her soft eyes glancing him reassurance that everything would work out for the best, even if it was clear their kids were headed out, leaving for colleges and cities and careers that would carry them far away forever. Farming was a hard, uncertain life anyway, and he couldn't think of a single good reason why they shouldn't go those other ways. Yet they had such a happy time of it, growing up under open skies, in safety and peace and plenty. Seemed to Will that's what they should want for their own kids.

So before they could get too worked up over it, when they were winding up their visit home at Christmastime and it was just the three of them, Will had made a speech. "Been thinking to sell off the place, here," he announced, in the even, quiet way he said things, large or small. "Get a little place over in Red Oak...take it easy." There was a long silence in the kitchen, Ruth splashing around in the dishes, Rizzy at her side, drying. They didn't even lift their heads, until Will thought maybe they hadn't understood what he'd said, or maybe hadn't heard him at all. Finally Rizzy, the young one, turned from the counter and stared at him hard, like she was having trouble seeing him, then she ran out of the room sobbing and Will said, "Well, good...I'm glad that's settled," which sent the other one running out too.

The lightning hit so close now that Will got up to see if the outbuildings were all right, then he stood with the curtain in his hand and wondered why it even mattered that they were. They didn't belong to him anymore anyhow.

He switched on the bedside light, sighed deeply, and said, "That's it. I may as well be up." He dressed and went downstairs, leaning pretty hard on the bannisters, half-asleep and still heavy from the fair portion of whiskey he'd had. It was usually dark when Will began his day, and he often walked through these familiar rooms without turning on lights, but he needed them now because there were cardboard boxes scattered everywhere, some full, others waiting to be packed. He put on coffee then sat at the dining room table, trying to clear his head.

A full-sized bureau drawer rested on the table beside him and in it lay a quarry of imponderables. Over the course of three generations, women of his family had done needlework using this drawer. Will had pulled from it a few things he thought were useful — needles, bobbins of thread, scissors — but he had no measure for the value of the rest. There were little practice pieces, the work of children and simple cross-stitch squares anyone could do. But crowded onto the right side of the drawer were piles of lace-work, the kind that Jenny had learned from Will's mother as a rite of passage to becoming a Hoffstetter.

As strong wind rattled the windowpanes, splashing sheets of rain against the north face of the house, Will pulled out all the lace works he could see and sorted them into piles. There were bracelets, cuffs and doilies, lots of squares five or six inches on a side, and one long strip a foot wide that may have been the beginning of a table runner from twenty or forty, maybe even sixty years ago, and never finished. There were rows of tiny flowers with nine petals each strung along vines with puffy clouds of white thread holding it all in place. He recalled asking Jenny how she ever had the patience for such things and for fun she made an effort to show him, placing the needle in one of his powerful hands and teaching him to pull loops off it with the tiny hook. He was hopeless and they had a laugh about it, but then she said seriously, "It's all about putting numbers into a thread, dear. It's just a thread tied into knots to form things. It's like anything else you make with your hands...only with lace, what makes it fun is that it's all one, long thread. See this square? To think, it's all one thread...one unbroken thread." Will had to admit it was pretty impressive.

"I'll be," he said, "who ever thought of that?"

"A spider did," she said, and went back to counting.

But the girls never took any interest in putting knots into a thread and when Will set the drawer out for them to look through, neither of them took anything from it to take back home with them. So what was any of it worth? Didn't all the work three generations of women put into it make it precious? What was the value of a farm — the land, the buildings, the machinery and all that had gone into it or come out of it — once your own flesh and blood had no use for it? As Will rose to get his coffee, these two things were all that he later could remember:

The electricity went off — which was not at all uncommon during rainstorms — and something happened to the air that made his ears pop and his spine tingle. "Whoa!' was all he got out before the bay windows blew away, sucking the air out of his lungs. He wheeled toward the door to the cellar steps, slammed into the dining room table hard enough to knock it over, pushing into an invisible hand that was forcing him back. With all his strength, he leaned toward the door, wrenched it open and got one shoe on the sill before flying into darkness.

* * *

Will had broken bones before and it was his first sensation, coming to. It was the other arm and some years ago, but he remembered how it ached and hung limp like this, before the onset of real pain. All was soaking wet, cold and totally dark where he was, but he reckoned he was still alive because every piece of him hurt too much to be dead. He began small, with working the fingers of his right hand, then the lower arm, the shoulder, touched his face and hair, sticky, matted with blood. Busted nose probably, but no serious concussion and so very cautiously, he turned himself over and sat up. Then he unbuttoned his shirt, shook it off his right arm, and rolled it into a twisted band around his useless left arm, wrapping the area above the wrist, hoping that both radius and ulna weren't broke like last time.

Sitting spread-legged on the floor in six inches of water, he waggled both feet, heartened to hear each splash in turn. He waved his good hand around tentatively, thumping into a post, a ledge, another, recognizing by feel his cellar stairway. There was generous pain in his back and ribs as he splashed cautiously up onto his knees, pulling with his right arm, but his body still worked, most of it. One-handed, it took a few minutes to pull off his belt, loop it through the shirt that was holding his left forearm together, buckle it and slip it over his head, but once his busted piece was in a sling, he could make it up the stairs, one by one, on his knees. It was best not to walk up the stairs in the dark anyway, since the top two steps and risers, just before the sill, were gone. Will lifted himself over this gap with difficulty, pushing against the third step with his legs and pulling on a table leg that, when he reached up, he found was the support leg of the spinet piano that used to be in the living room.

It was raining heavily in the dining room, or rather on the floor that had been in the dining room. Will drew himself slowly to his feet and tilted his face skyward, letting the rain tell him what he still could not see — that there was no longer a house at the top of the cellar stairs. The wet wind blew straight through what was left of the house his grandfather had built, his father had expanded, he had modernized.

Will was working his way carefully across the debris by feel, trying to get clear of the wreckage before some electric company fool tried to improve his life by restoring power, when the lights of a pickup bounced off the gravel roadway. Without a word, his neighbor's teenage sons jumped out and ran over to help him in the glare of the headlights. One gently cradled a wrapped-up arm as they tiptoed through the ruins toward the truck, then they stood close by the light and looked it over. The adrenaline drained away from Will; now that he was out of danger, the pain set in sharp and his legs went weak.

The older boy placed his good arm under Will's bad one for support and carefully unwound the soaked shirt. "Find us a splint, Donny, two pieces," he ordered. "This all you got broke, Mr. Hofstetter?"

"I guess," Will said, hoping he was right.

"What's this for?" he asked. Will squinted into the glare of the headlamp to see the boy pull a soaked, wadded square of lace out of his limp hand.

"Oh, that..." Will told him, "that's a keepsake." The look on the boy's face clearly showed admiration for the toughness of the old man, but he didn't say anything as he flattened the piece onto the hood of the pickup, folded it in half, and poked it into the hip pocket of Will's jeans.

The boys walked with him into the emergency room in Red Oak, right at dawn, but when they offered to wait with him, he sent them on home.

"Appreciate your help, fellas, but I reckon I live here in town now," he told them. "The Good Lord in His wisdom is all finished with that farm..." He paused and swallowed hard. "I've got to be, too."

i

Where Monsters Lay

Jess M. Collette

I t came between the laughter. That curious sound from deep in the forest, haunting and enigmatic that made Sis and me stop and stare into each other's eyes. Inside Sis's eyes were questions, excitement, and pools of anticipation tinged with fear. I suspect she saw the same deep inside of mine. There was silence but a moment before Sis's laughter, hesitant and choppy, ignited mine.

"That was the loudest we've heard yet!" Sis whispered. Her hand shook slightly as she reached to tuck a loose strand of my auburn hair, frizzy from the humidity, behind one of my protruding ears. My big, dumb ears, oh how I hated them! The hair Sis placed behind one seemed to hate them, too. It refused to stay put, instead bouncing wild and free on the sporadic summer breeze. "That's got to be the closest we've heard from the monster Davey warned us about!" I shivered as I heard the steely truth of my big Sis's words. Every word that had left our older brother Davey's mouth last summer rushed back to me. My head spun, realizing words of warning are always hard to forget. Davey's words, I have never forgotten.

"It's big," he'd said. "How big, you ask? Great-grandpop said it's bigger than the Christmas pine, you know the one he planted when he bought this land! But he also said it's not always big. The monster comes in many forms. Sometimes it's covered in thick hairs that are just as prickly as the old Christmas pine! Or it can be mechanical, like the huge locomotive that runs on fire and blows smoke as it rushes through town. And other times, well, other times it can be in its most dangerous form. Beware of the monsters that look like you or me."

We listened intently as Davey retold the legend our great-grandpop had passed down over the years, Sis with her eyes wide, me chewing my nails to stubs, one by one. I didn't even see Sis blink once, and I never took my eyes off her. I stared and blew away bits of chewed-off nail that had stuck to my chapped lips. In silence we listened, mesmerized by the tale Davey told as if it was all brand-new.

Davey's gaze bounced from Sis to me and back again. His shoulders dropped, one corner of his mouth turned up and his voice became airy and playful. "Let us always remember the legend great-grandpop passed down himself that says with just one prick from the Christmas pine monster's poison needle-like hair, you'll be seeing all kinds of things that aren't even there! But before you see it, you'll hear it. You'll hear a foul, haunting howl. It will come from somewhere deep in the woods; nowhere, yet everywhere is this guttural, echoing call. When you hear it, well, that's the impending start of it all!"

Davey played out the tale with his hands and arms that sticky day last summer just before the storm clouds moved in. Beneath our innocent laughter, thunder clapped in the distance, an ominous warning that seamlessly transitioned the innocence of my big brother's words. Although it wasn't the first time we'd heard the legend, Davey's words were the same but different. Davey spoke about the legend like he might never speak about it again. I listened like I finally knew what my big dumb ears were good for. I tucked away every single word Davey gave me.

"But, girls, there is no need to be worried about the monsters. Great-grandpop also said how to tame them. Lucky for you, your big brother is in on that secret." We leaned in closer to hear the secret Davey had to tell. As he bent down to our level, I locked eyes with his. His eyes were wells, holding details miles deep. His pursed lips were ready to divulge the truths he held. His words cradled the questions running through my thoughts. "Secrets aren't secrets if they're told. I will protect you both from mysteries the forest and the world holds."

Davey finished telling us the legend by pulling out his guitar. We lost his gaze to the emerging starry night. Worlds away, he strummed the strings. One after the other, they sang out into the dusky night. Each note delivered a permission slip for the sun to set a little deeper into the horizon. I held Sis's hand as we sat on the old tree stump, wet and spongy, both staring into the darkening forest. The trees seemed to dance to the melody Davey plucked. Soon, the darkness didn't seem so dark. Fireflies ignited and sputtered from limb to limb, their lights flashing in time with the soothing notes that floated from guitar to air.

"This, girls, is how you tame the monsters!" With a mischievous smile on his face, somewhere between full toothy and puckered lips, Davey never stopped playing as he told us Great-grandpop's secret. "This guitar was his and has been passed down through the family. It's been with me for a few years, and I'd like to share it with both of you. If ever I'm not here, just pick up this guitar and strum. Strum until your heart is full and the forest is silenced. Strum as soon as you hear the monster's howl and continue to play until the forest dances. The notes don't matter, it's all about the intention of the fingers doing the strumming!"

He had Sis and me run our fingers across the strings. The cold metal was stiff against the supple skin on my fingertips. The strings sprung back under my slightest touch and released fantastic sounds, dispersing the heaviness of the night air. I felt empowered knowing Great-grandpop's secret. As I rubbed the indentation left by the strings on my fingertip, I watched Sis do the same. Our dented fingers would fade away, but Davey's words made an indelible mark for always.

Now, as we remembered Davey's words, Sis and I knew exactly what we needed to do in response to hearing the monster. "Let's get Davey's guitar, Sis." Sis grabbed my hand as we ran through the clumps of overgrown grass sprinkled with wildflowers. We ran all the way to the hay barn and slid open the creaky door that hung on rusty tracks. It wailed but a moment, begrudgingly leaving us just enough space to squeeze inside. To the right of the door, hanging on an extra-long nail, was Davey's guitar. Although last summer he said it wasn't just his but all of ours, to Sis and me it would always be his. His name carved deep into the wood said so. Sis climbed up on a haybale, making her just tall enough to reach the shoulder strap from tippy-toed feet. She gently lowered down the guitar case, which was decorated in worn and peeling stickers. The edges of the largest one, a multi-colored peace sign, tickled the palm of my hand.

Over grass mounds we ran, sneezing from ragweed until we were back at the uneven edge of the forest. With two clicks, Sis opened the case. The old tree stump, still spongy and damp, gave us a place to sit with the guitar lying flat on Sis's lap. We took turns plucking the tightly pulled strings. Though the wire was hard and brittle, it still sang out a soothing song. We played and played until the forest transformed, just as Davey had said it would. As the trees danced and swayed, their leaves added percussion to our song, lulling the lightning bugs out of their beds. Before our eyes, the night transformed. It felt safe and nearly complete.

One thing was missing. One very important, obvious part of our world was missing. Sis and I ran our fingers over the carving on the guitar. Our fingers traced out *Davey*. It was that same day last summer when he told us, "The military needs my help fighting monsters." His words had stung, taking my breath away. A single tear had trickled down Sis's freckled cheek. "Don't worry girls, I've received all I'll ever need right here on this land. Right here in our forest is where my heart will always be, even when I can't be. It's not so bad when you know how to tame monsters," he said. "Great-grandpop, Grandpop, Dad, me, and now you, we all learned the secret of how to tame monsters right here on this very land, with this same guitar. It has transformative powers that can make everyone stop and listen. Then, maybe just maybe, there is a chance for change. Promise me one thing, girls, never stop strumming," Davey asked of us just before he had left. "Promise me you'll play a tune to lead me back home." As Sis and I touched the guitar, it vibrated with history. It was their history, Davey's history, our history. It was a history that ran throughout our land and found its way home through our veins.

I wondered if Sis or I would be called to fight monsters one day. I knew that day might very well come, but right now I knew we had plenty of time to wonder. Right now, we had a promise to keep and a guitar to play. Davey's words rushed back to me from somewhere stored inside my big dumb ears. "When the tune is just right, they'll be no need to tame, fight, or defeat monsters any longer. One day they'll only be the stuff of legends. No one has found the right tune to make that happen just yet, but when someone does, and they surely will, we'll all be transported to a land where monsters lay. In that land all the monsters will fall fast asleep, never to wake from their slumber. In that land, we'll all be free to dream new dreams."

Mixed with the whimsical notes we created on the guitar I heard the repeated thud of approaching footsteps, followed by a voice that for so long only spoke within my head. I saw Sis's eyes the size of saucers and I knew she'd heard it too! In expectant disbelief, we turned to see him. "Girls, I see you've never stopped strumming," Davey said with smiling eyes. I jumped up and ran toward my big brother with Sis right behind me clipping my heels. I wrapped my arms around him, and Sis did the same right above mine. In our embrace, Davey trembled. It was a deep shaking not visible but easily felt. As he spoke, I heard the tremble and then felt it fade and fall away. He let out a deep breath and his words came more smoothly. "You know, girls, the thought of our time together with this guitar and the tunes I knew you'd be playing when I was gone, brought me home." Davey walked to the spongy stump and reached for the guitar. As he swung the shoulder strap over his head, Sis and I sat on the ground, our legs crossed, and our chins propped up by our hands and elbows. Davey plucked a few chords and then looked down at Sis and me. They were still there, maybe a little more in the distance, but the stars still sparkled in his eyes. "Since I was a lucky one to make it back home, maybe together, we can be the lucky ones to find the tune that tames the monsters. Maybe together, we can find the tune the whole world needs."

The Geometry of Imaginary Spaces

K. Eric Crook

As I breathlessly scanned the Departures Board it clearly said 10:18 – but halfway down the screen it just as clearly admitted that my flight had departed at least two minutes early. So began my night in Detroit-Metro Airport, ending my quest to find a poem fitting the title of a study I saw referenced in a biography of Nobel Prize-winning mathematician John Nash.

And what could be more imaginary than being stranded in Detroit in the dead of night with a handful of other disgruntled wayfarers who, like me, were victimized by the random appearance of a herd of thunderstorms rampaging across the Midwest? But of course, you are entirely correct, this could not be a random event unless all events are, at heart, random.

Well then, are they imaginary? It can be shown that you can define a cone of infinite depth that can never be completely filled with water, or rum, which would have been handy right now. But these thoughts are not based on that. No, I confess that I have been drawn to this concept, the geometry of imaginary spaces, because it so aptly describes the impermanence of being.

We assume that what we see is real, but it is nothing more immutable than cognition. If flight 1921 had not departed early, my reality would be domiciled in seat 23B, homeward bound. But this strays from the point: how can we define reality based on our perceptions? If you can define the form and geometry of imaginary space within an equation, isn't this all imaginary?

It is past midnight now in Detroit-Metro Airport. The maintenance workers are buffing the floors, preparing the facility for my rejoinder with reality tomorrow morning, when I board the first flight to Providence. They throw you a smile, glad to see that you've had this opportunity to see the reality of their lives. They are the guardians of this imaginary scene.

But for the construct of time we could be doomed to repeat these moments indefinitely – the maintenance worker rides by mounted on the buffing machine, he smiles in my direction, I wave back, I look down at the rough draft of the words I am composing on this page, only to be distracted by the maintenance worker smiling in my direction again, yet again, and again.

So here we all are, a handful of actors playing our roles in a grade-B movie, while the director yells cut and has us run the scene again and again, until we get it right. It is nothing more compelling than an existential movie, but without the sex, without the drama, without dialogue. It is truly imaginary, staged in the stark geometry of countless airports, now playing, forever.

Lord knows how I slept wedged on a bench no wider than a church pew; my entire body ached. The cold I caught sleeping rough is still with me now - proof, it would seem, that I have not imagined all this. My flight to Providence the next morning was an hour late departing. Delta has sent me numerous e-mails telling me that they value my feedback. I will send them this.

Life Cycle

Mary Wheeler

Everyone has gone; friends who gathered, sisters, brothers, children – a son,
a daughter.
Each returning to the life they know away from here.

I wander through the house making little adjustments.
Everything is clean, but still I settle things in exactly the right place,

Finally, I sit – really alone after 33 years.

The silence engulfs me except for the songs spooling in my head.
Songs written so many years ago telling of love, joy, hope, expectation.

So many memories, each a reminder of the life we shared.
All treasured moments – laughter, happiness, anger, irritation, bitterness,
loss.

Days pass and finally spring returns, breathing new life into everything it
surrounds.
Just as the garden renews and shares its beauty; fresh and alive, a reminder
of rebirth.

Just as the rose on the other side of the wall, unseen, like him.
But blooming as beautiful and fragrant as if present for my eyes.

A new sense of purpose awakens; finally returning to the world with new
perspective.
Coat of overwhelming responsibility shed, and once again,
Renewed hope for a life unfolding with unexpected joy, love, and happiness.

About the Authors

Rick Billings has been an artist and writer ever since he can remember. Throughout his years as a food service manager, and later as a firefighter/EMT, Rick maintained his passion for the arts and continued to develop his talents. He has self-published two children's books – *The Tragic Tale of Mr. Moofs* and *Melba Blue*, as well as an anthology of his firefighting-related cartoons over twenty years – *Who Took my Toast? and other tales of the firehouse*.... He is hard at work on a sequel to *Mr. Moofs*.

Rick lives in Barrington, Rhode Island with his wife and Nala the wonder dog.

"I really enjoy the process of writing and illustrating children's books. There is a lot of freedom regarding subjects and art disciplines which leaves the field open to anything that I can imagine. 'Two Twains on a Train' came about after a silly discussion that I had with a friend. It was one of those things that just came pouring out once I began. I love that it comes across in a Suess-like rhythm. I am still intending to illustrate it but am trying to determine the best style that will suit the story."

David Boiani is an author of psychological thrillers living in Coventry, Rhode Island. Discovering Stephen King at an early age sparked his desire to read and he quickly moved on to other genres. He also plays guitar in an alternative rock band that writes its own original music.

"I have been writing for five years. I have four books published with two more due for release in the next year. My inspiration comes from wanting to connect with my readers, entertain them, make them feel emotion. Ultimately, I believe that is what art is: the ability to make someone feel emotion.

"I have released two psychological thrillers: *A Thin Line* and *The Redemption*, its sequel. I have also published two collections: *Dark Musings* and *Darker Musings*, which include stories from a mix of genres - horror, thriller and suspense, mystery, science fiction, legend, and historical fiction. I enjoy experimenting with my writing, which is why I enjoy creating short stories; there is a freedom present that you do not encounter writing novels. I have recently branched out into multiple genres I had yet to explore and hope to continue to broaden my craft and scope."

Judy Boss is the author of two novels, *Deception Island*, a suspense novel set in Antarctica, and *Fall from Grace*, a mystery set in Rhode Island, as well as four college textbooks published by McGraw-Hill Higher Education. For more information please visit her website at www.judyboss.com.

"I have been writing and illustrating stories since I was a child and have made my living as a writer most of my adult life. In addition to my novels and short stories (which do *not* support me financially), I worked as a researcher/writer for the Nova Scotia Museum in Canada for several years following graduate school and later as a textbook writer for McGraw-Hill Higher Education. I am currently working on the fifth edition of my critical thinking textbook, *THiNK.*

Pamela Carey graduated with a B.A. from Colby College and an M.A. from Columbia University Teachers College. She taught high school English in Connecticut, Georgia, and Maine, before obtaining an M.A. from Rhode Island School of Design and opening her own interior design firm.

As a child she wrote mushy poems while sitting on a bridge over a brook at her home in Connecticut. As a high school English teacher, mother of two sons in the Red Sox organization, and world traveler, she began keeping journals. The journals transformed into three books of nonfiction: *Minor League Mom: A Mother's Journey through the Red Sox Farm Teams, Elderly Parents with All Their Marbles: A Survival Guide for the Kids,* and *Surviving Your Dream Vacation: 75 Rules to Keep Your Companion Talking to You on the Road.*

When not writing, reading for her book clubs, or traveling, Pam can be found on the tennis court as a member of two South Palm Beach County tennis teams. She and her husband reside in Delray Beach, Florida, and in Westport, Massachusetts.

A. Keith Carreiro earned his master's and doctoral degrees from Harvard Graduate School of Education. His academic focus, including his ongoing research agenda, centers around philosophically

148

examining how creativity and critical thinking are acquired, learned, utilized, and practiced in the literary, visual, and performing arts. He has taken his findings and applied them to the professional development of educational practitioners and other creative artists.

Due to A. Keith Carreiro's love of family, he has seen his fervor for history, as well as his passion for wondering about the future, deepen dramatically.

He lives in Swansea, Massachusetts and has six children and 14 grandchildren. He belongs to an eighty–five–pound golden retriever and an impish Calico cat.

In 2014, he began writing the first manuscript of a science fiction/fantasy thriller in a series called *The Immortality Wars*. It is a cautionary tale about the quest for human immortality. The first trilogy, of a planned three trilogy series, was released on his 71st birthday.

"The genres I write in are science fiction/fantasy and nonfiction. I am also working on a thriller mystery novel idea that takes place in East Providence in the late summer of 1954. Throw in a little bit of Dean Koontz, Stephen King, and Lee Child with J. R. R. Tolkien and C. S. Lewis, and I am happy to say that these writers are my heroes who inspire me to write stories that enchant, terrify, and hopefully entertain my readers."

R.N. Chevalier is a veteran of the Army and Air Force who was diagnosed with ALS in March of 2012.

Since his diagnosis, Chevalier has published a sci-fi trilogy: *Are We the Klingons, Advances of the Ancients,* and *Full Circle.*

He has also published a photo book, *Rhode Island Civil War Monuments – A Pictorial Guide*, which he co-authored with his wife Donna, and a children's sci-fi book, *Jay and Rowan-In Time*, which was illustrated by his daughter Jasmine.

Jess M. Collette has always called New England home. She has lived in Massachusetts, Vermont, and Rhode Island. The beauty and ever-changing seasons in this region inspire her writing. In addition to nature, Jess also writes about love and loss, drawing from her own experience of losing her only child, Joshua. In his honor, she has published two books. In addition to writing, she also makes unique creations with graphic design. She lives in Rhode Island with her husband and their adorable rescue dog from Texas. Visit www.jessicamcollette.com for updates and to view current writing, poetry, and designs.

"I have always loved to write. Whether for an assignment, something special for a family member or just for fun, I've filled many a page. It wasn't until the loss of my son Joshua that I was inspired to write and publish the children's book on grieving, *Your Special Star*. Shortly after, I published my debut novel, *Naming the Bits Between*, an uplifting fictional adventure about the cycle of life: loss, discovery, and finding renewed purpose.

"The tagline on my website is *Fictional Sentiments Inspired by Life*. That really does sum it all up... I write works of fiction and poetry based on what I've experienced and the nuggets of truth I've found along the journey. I love to meld the physical and spiritual worlds together, so always look for hidden meanings in my writing. I enjoy pairing a photo I've taken with a poem or poetic short story I've written. Most recently, I've been making compilation pieces of my writing and graphic design. There's always something new to write about when you aim to see the extraordinary in the ordinary. After all, isn't life more fun that way? I think so. I try to live and write from a positive perspective. My hope is to see and learn something new every day!"

Kevin Duarte's biography consists of numerous stories written in high school and college as a fine arts minor at Roger Williams University. He had a poem published in the college anthology when he was a senior.

In his late twenties, a local company produced a comic book called "P.R.I.M.E.," which Duarte wrote with a friend. Duarte came up with the main idea, and his friend, as the illustrator, helped fine-tune the concept and illustrated the comic. The comic was produced and sold quite well in the local area, garnering local TV coverage at one of the book signings in a local comic book store.

Duarte is currently working on a novel called *Manifest Destiny* and has completed the first draft. He hopes to have it completed by the end of 2019.

"I've been inspired by the likes of Ray Bradbury, H. G. Wells, J.R.R. Tolkien, and Chris Claremont. Rod Serling and *The Twilight Zone* have been a major source of inspiration as his works are about as timeless as they get. Another source of inspiration were the many classic authors that were part of the creative writing curriculum at Roger Williams University. If not for this course of study, I would not have read and become engaged by many of the classic works of literature such as *The Great Gatsby*, *War of the Worlds*, and *Heart of Darkness*, to name a few.

"I love writing speculative science fiction, as well as fantasy. I am inspired by the possibilities of the human collective, both good and bad, and love to create characters as much as I love to create and modify the world around them."

At 66, **K. Eric Crook** has worked as a carpenter, laborer, machinist, forester, instructor, and financial advisor. But his avocation is writing, the rest is just about paying the bills. He is currently working on a trilogy loosely based on his experiences working as a forester. But then there are also short stories to be completed, poems to write, prose that seems to come out of nowhere, and countless other avenues to be explored.

Hank Ellis is a retired environmental scientist with degrees in natural resources and wildlife management. He is the author of *The Promise: A Perilous Journey,* a YA-to-adult action-adventure story of two young brothers.

This unpublished piece is part of a sequel to *The Promise: A Perilous Journey.*

Dean Fachon has been a resident of East Greenwich for many years and grew up sailing on Narragansett Bay and the Cape. He graduated from Colgate University with a bachelor's degree in English, then studied technical writing at Rensselaer Polytechnic Institute. He worked for IBM and Digital Equipment Corporation before becoming one of the first web site developers in the country. He later became a communications consultant, writing success stories and PR-related materials for a variety of companies. He's been married to Wendy for 25 years and they have a daughter, Evie.

"I'm inspired to seek the truth and share my insights. I have been writing for many decades. Most of my published work is technical, along with a variety of articles and political commentary, but I have long desired to indulge my more creative impulses."

Jill Fague grew up as a middle child, developing an independent spirit. She now enjoys her career as an English teacher, and not surprisingly, she relates well to some of her more spirited students. While she maintains a close relationship with her brother, who no longer tries to kill her on a regular basis, her younger sister claims the title as her best friend. Married for nineteen years, Jill lives with her husband and two teenage children. The most recent addition to her family is an adopted, spotted tiger kitten born with plenty of spunk.

"When my grandfather died in 2012, I realized that all the tales he loved to tell went to the grave with him. I wish I had recorded them, instead of feeling impatient each time I heard a rerun. During a battle with cancer seven years ago, I felt compelled to document my own journey. Desperation and boredom kept me writing during my year-long treatment plan. Some of my moments and funny flashbacks turned into my memoir, *This Unfamiliar Road*, published two years ago. Around that time, I began speaking at American Cancer Society events, and I have donated proceeds from the sale of my book to this important mission.

"Memoir writing appeals to me because I can bring significant moments back to life. My words have the power to preserve family accounts with a personal touch. I miss my late mother, and I would love to hold a book told in her unique voice. This is a gift I can leave my children."

Marjorie Turner Hollman lives next to Silver Lake in Bellingham, Massachusetts. When she isn't paddling her little red kayak, or walking, she can be found at home writing, reading, or cooking. Her newest "steed" (another surprise) is a foot-forward, adaptive tandem bike, which she rides all over New England with her husband.

A personal historian, Turner Hollman is the author of multiple personal histories (private memoirs), and several books in the "Easy Walks in Massachusetts" trail book series. She has been writing professionally for more than twenty years. Visit her website at www.MarjorieTurner.com

Turner Hollman grew up in Florida and comes from a long line of southern storytellers. Her degree in history is from Bridgewater State College. She was beckoned north by college—and snow! Listening to family stories makes her heart sing.

Sam Kafrissen was born and raised in West Warwick and later Cranston, Rhode Island. He now lives in Arlington, Massachusetts. Since 2014, he has published three Doherty mystery novels: *The Mill Town*, *The Lost Survivor*, and *The Missing Films*. A fourth book, *The Girl on the Rocks*, is due to be published next spring. All of his novels are set in various parts of Rhode Island in the late 1950s-early 1960s. In addition to these books, Kafrissen has had short stories printed in several anthologies including *Selections* (2018). He has had numerous stories published in his hometown newspaper, *The Arlington Advocate* and in the *Provincetown Banner* on Cape Cod.

"Class Day" is a semi-fictional account of a ninth-grade class day celebration. It is one of nearly thirty short stories and memoir pieces Kafrissen has written for two writing groups since 2008. A number of them are reflections of incidents he witnessed or participated in when he was young. Some of them have been embellished for the purposes of drama or entertainment.

"As with most of my short writings, this is a fictional short story. However, I try for the most part to set them in real places surrounded by real events, to which I then add dramatic slants. All of my memoir-style stories are sprinkled with elements of nostalgia, often relating to a Rhode Island of the past."

Paul Lonardo has had both fiction and nonfiction books published, including numerous collaborative titles. He studied filmmaking and screenwriting at Columbia College Hollywood, earned an A.S. in Mortuary Science from Mount Ida College and a B.A. in English from the University of Rhode Island. He is a freelance writer and author, and lives in Lincoln, Rhode Island with his wife and son.

"I have been writing in one form or another for most of my life. Creatively, my first love was filmmaking and screenwriting. As a teen, I made several films on Super-8. Yes, Super-8. Video was available at the time, but super low-budget was the reason for this choice of medium. I transitioned into writing science fiction/horror (it was the 1980s), mostly short stories, but my first published book was a sci-fi/horror novel, *The Apostate*. Since then, I have had more than a dozen books published, half through traditional publishers/agents, the others self-published, with most of this variety being collaborations with individuals who I helped tell personal stories in the autobiography and memoir genres. I've had everything from true crime books to romance novellas published, and my inspirations run the gamut, as do my titles. My latest published work, *The New Debtors' Prison*, as published in May 2019. This nonfiction work details the custodial perils of debt in modern society. It was co-written with Rhode Island attorney and former state senator who spent two years in federal prison for bank fraud.

Paul Magnan has been writing fiction that veers from the straight and narrow for many years. He has had many short stories published, and his collection, *Veering From the Straight and Narrow*, is available from Amazon.

Magnan's influences run from Poe to Bradbury to Lovecraft, and to the Twilight Zone and back. Horror, dark fantasy, surrealism, anything that's speculative and off the beaten path is of interest to him.

He has gleefully explored the dark and cold corners of his mind and come back with stories that, hopefully, takes the reader by surprise and makes them think. Characters need to be real, but their worlds, and what they face in it, are wide open and very shadowy.

Jack Nolan grew up in northern Indiana, where he worked for a time, like his father and grandfather, for United States Steel, Gary Works. An undergraduate degree from Ball State University punched his ticket for a three-year hitch with Army Intelligence from 1967 to 1970, during which time he was stationed at Fort Holabird, then on civilian status in Can Tho and Saigon, then at Fort Meade, training others. A doctorate in history from Columbia University opened the door to many happy years of teaching college-bound students at University High School, Tucson, where he taught AP American literature and AP European history.

Nolan lives with his wife Patricia in Providence, where he is finishing a sequel to his 2017 comic novel about coming of age in the 1960s, *Vietnam Remix*.

"My story 'Final Harvest' was inspired by the farm families I grew up with in Northern Indiana. They're from a tough, no-nonsense, God-fearing culture, in pretty sharp contrast to the steelworkers' kids that shared the same high school. This is my tribute to them. I've been writing seriously since 1984 and have finished three novels, one of which I published last year – *Vietnam Remix* - based on my experiences with Army Intelligence in Saigon. VR is not a 'war' book, but a comic take on coming of age in that exotic setting.

"I have written dozens of short stories meant to stretch my skills and imagination. I enjoy writing about people on the fringes of society (see "Castaway" in the 2018 anthology *Selections*) and I favor storytelling that has a beginning, middle and end."

Joanne Perella is smitten with life. Her writing is a product of her love for the people, places, things, and events she encounters day to day, week to week, and year to year. She sees the big things in little moments.

A lifelong resident of Rhode Island, she is currently working on her first novel. This is her third story to be published in an ARIA anthology.

Steven R. Porter is the author of two novels: the critically-acclaimed Southie crime thriller *Confessions of the Meek and the Valiant*, and the award-winning historical novel *Manisses,* inspired by the rich history of Block Island. He is also the co-author of *Scared to Death...Do It Anyway,* a guide for individuals who suffer from anxiety and panic attacks.

Porter speaks frequently to schools and libraries about his books, trends in independent publishing, and on special topics in writing and book marketing. He served as Director of Advertising and Public Relations for the 176-store Lauriat's bookstore chain through the 1990s, and today, he and his wife Dawn own Stillwater Books and the independent press, Stillwater River Publications, in Pawtucket, Rhode Island. He is founder and president of the Association of Rhode Island Authors (ARIA).

Porter has been writing fiction, poetry, satire, and commentary since the late 1980s when he was editor of the University of Rhode Island's award-winning literary magazine *The Great Swamp Gazette.* Although he admits that poetry is not his first love, he has accumulated many pieces over the years that he intends to publish in an anthology sometime next year. *A Hymn for a Memory* was inspired by the idea that while specific details of events fade as we age, feelings don't.

Rick Roberts is a veteran of Boston's advertising community, the Orvis fly fishing school, and the United States Army. He was educated at Lehigh University, the University of Iowa, and Harvard. He has written two books: *I Was Much Happier When Everything I Owned was in the Back Seat of my Volkswagen,* a nonfiction boomer rant, and *Digital Darling,* a novel pitching three revolutionaries against the NSA in an Internet war. He lives in Bristol.

Theresa Schimmel is the author of the adult novel *Braided Secrets* and four children's books: *Sunny, The Circus Song, The Carousel Adventure,* and *David's War/David's Peace.* Her short stories and poems have been featured and won awards in literary magazines and newspaper. *Braided Secrets* is her debut adult/young adult novel. She is a member of the Association of Rhode Island Authors.

After twenty-six years of classroom teaching experience, Schimmel worked as an early childhood educational consultant at the state and national levels. Now, most of her free time is spent writing. Married with two adult sons and two grandchildren, she resides in Rhode Island with her husband Steve. Her books can be purchased through www.tamstales.net . Some are also available through www.amazon.com and local bookstores.

Mike Squatrito has been writing *The Overlords* series for over twenty years. Currently, he lives in Tiverton, Rhode Island with his wife Lea and their children, Devin and Samantha. Mike speaks at elementary, middle, and high schools, colleges, local libraries, and writers' groups, where his sincere hope is to inspire everyone he meets to be creative and follow their dreams. He also is the Vice President of the Association of Rhode Island Authors (ARIA).

When not working on the *Overlords* series, Mike is active in fitness and sports. He is a knuckleball pitcher for the Narragansett Brewers, a team that won the 2008 and 2014 National Championships in Phoenix, Arizona. He also runs four to five miles on a regular basis, does interval weight and cardio training, and takes Vinyasa yoga classes twice a week. Plus, he's an engineer, working on Homeland Defense projects.

"I've been writing for over 25 years, predominately working on my *Overlords* fantasy book series. I have three books in the series in print with the fourth, and final, book released in the fall of 2019. My inspiration for writing is to hopefully let people escape into my worlds and leave their daily grind behind. I'm looking to broaden my literary horizons by writing more science fiction, as well as a baseball memoir in the near future. I write mostly fantasy, though this submission is science fiction."

Anne-Marie Sutton has been writing since she joined the staff of her middle school newspaper. A graduate of the University of Maryland with a degree in English, she has held posts in journalism, marketing, and public relations. She has taught mass communication at the college level and also worked as a political consultant in Connecticut.

"In my business career, I had to follow assignments given by others. Later in life I was able to turn my efforts to creative writing. I decided on writing mysteries as I have always enjoyed reading the classic detective stories and whodunits. In 2004, I published my first Newport mystery, *Murder Stalks* a *Mansion*. Set in contemporary times, it was inspired by Agatha Christie. Three more books have followed, including the latest, *Invest in Death*. I also enjoy writing short stories and have had my work published in anthologies from Darkhouse Books, in two Sisters In Crime "Murder In New York" collections, and in "Rogue Wave: The Best New England Crime Stories 2015" from Level Best Books; and also a short mystery story set New-port online at Mysterical-E.

"While doing book signings for my Newport Mystery series I am frequently asked if I have written any ghost stories. While I have had to say that I have not, "The Boy in the Window" represents my first story in this genre. The house in the setting and its schoolroom were inspired by a visit to the Ward-Heitmann Museum House in West Haven, Connecticut. The plot and the characters are fictional."

Debbie Kaiman Tillinghast is the author of *The Ferry Home*, a memoir about her childhood on Prudence Island, a tiny island off the coast of Rhode Island. She began writing as she embarked on a quest to reconnect with her island roots, starting with a cookbook for her family. A retired teacher and nutrition educator, she now enjoys volunteering as well as writing, gardening, biking, and spending time with her children and grandchildren.

"After my first book, *The Ferry Home*, was published in 2015, I continued to write stories and poetry about my life, my family, and nature. I have also been published in *Country* magazine, and in three anthologies published by the Association of Rhode Island Authors: *Shoreline, Under the 13th Star,* and *Selections*.

On Prudence Island, daily existence was guided by the changing seasons and the tides. Perhaps because of my island childhood, my senses are tuned to the world around me, and I still feel bound to island life. Whether I'm writing a poem or an essay, my stories focus on the moments in my life that touch me, a poignant memory, the birds outside my window, or the silence of a winter day."

Mary Wheeler came to the writing table late in life, but it's become a new, fun career. She has published one children's book (*Twirling and Dancing with Annie and Friends*), and the second one (*Home in the Beech Tree*) was released in the fall of 2019. Writing children's stories is her main focus, but a few poems and larger works have wormed their way into her writing menu. She looks forward to writing as themes inspire her, and spending time with family and friends in beautiful New England.

"I usually find inspiration for new stories when I'm walking outside. A look or a glance at something along the path triggers a thought, then a book idea. I envision the story in my mind and how it might spin out. It's so much fun. I've been writing for only a couple of years but have enough story ideas to last a lifetime.

"I currently write children's stories but have also begun work on two novels. I began writing because a classroom assignment required giving a home-made gift to a classmate. The first book was the result. I plan to expand my writing to include other kinds of works, including poems, mysteries, and historical novels."

Barbara Ann Whitman is a seasoned social worker with experience as a child abuse and neglect investigator. She has worked professionally with hundreds of foster children. Currently, she is employed by a nonprofit agency that empowers foster children to become successful adults.

She has been a Sunday school teacher, a youth group leader, a parenting instructor, a Big Sister, and a Girl Scout Leader. She founded a Meetup group for active seniors in 2015. A member of the Old Fiddlers Club of Rhode Island, she also serves as an officer. Whitman sings in her church choir and belongs to a Celtic music group. She helps facilitate a writers' group at the local library.

"My writing falls across many genres, including the following published works: *Have Mercy* is a young adult/crossover novel about a young woman's journey from the foster care system to adulthood. 'A Changing Sea' is a love story/fiction (included in the 2016 anthology, *Shoreline*). 'Galilee' is a poem published in the 2017 ARIA anthology, *Under the 13th Star*), and 'A Crown of Diamonds' is a children's story, written to empower young girls (included in the 2018 anthology *Selections*).

Whitman also developed a blog at www.rhodiebean.com and, a member of the Yelp Elite squad, writes reviews of various restaurants and local businesses.

ORDER FORM

Please use the following to order additional copies of

Selections (2018), Under the 13th Star (2017), and/or *Shoreline* (2016)
Selected Short Fiction, Nonfiction, Poetry and Prose from The Association of Rhode Island Authors

_____ (QTY) **Past, Present, and Future**X $10.00 Total $_____
_____ (QTY) **Selections**   X $15.00 Total $_____
_____ (QTY) **Under the 13th Star**   X $10.00 Total $_____
_____ (QTY) **Shoreline**   X $10.00 Total $_____

**Shipping & Handling $_____

GRAND TOTAL $_____

**Shipping & Handling: Please add $3.00 for the first copy, and $1.50 for each additional copy.

Payment Method:

___ Personal Check Enclosed (Payable to ARIA)

___ Charge my Credit Card

Name:_____ BILLING ZIP CODE:_____

Visa____MC_____Amex_____ Discover____

Card Number:_____ EXP:_____/_____CSC_____

Signature:_____

Ship To:

Name _____

Street _____

City _____State:_____Zip:_____

Phone _____Email:_____

___Check to add to ARIA's email list.

MAIL YOUR COMPLETED FORM TO:
The Association of Rhode Island Authors (ARIA)
c/o Stillwater River Publications
63 Sawmill Road
Chepachet, RI 02814
info@stillwaterpress.com
www.StillwaterPress.com
www.RIAuthors.org